WHY TEACH?

A NOVEL

PETER SHULL

LOWER MIDLIST PUBLISHING, LLC

Cover design by Nathaniel Roy.

Cover art sketch by Maurice Olin.

For my teachers

"Now what I want is Facts. Teach these
boys and girls nothing but Facts. Facts alone
are what is wanted in life. Plant nothing else,
root out everything else. . . . Stick to Facts, sir!"
-Charles Dickens, *Hard Times*

"As good almost kill a man as kill a good book:
Who kills a man kills a reasonable creature, God's image;
but he who destroys a good book kills reason itself."
-John Milton, *Areopagitica*

"Or you can always go to law school
if things don't work out"
-Taylor Mali, "What Teachers Make"

PART I

1

This was a little after eleven o'clock, the night of the funeral, Davis, Garret, and me alone at a table at the back of the High Plains Oasis.

"You guys are good shits," Davis said, his elbows collapsing beneath him.

"Well," I said.

"Really good shits," he said, and then he put his head down among the empty glasses and half-killed bottles and began to snore.

"That one of the new ones from your department?" Garret asked. He had been looking off toward the floor where a group of underage girls with black-markered X's on their hands had been dancing, so I glanced there.

"No—" He redirected my gaze with a nod of his head. "Over at that table with the grade school teachers. Looking this way."

I looked across the bar. "It is." She wore a critical expression as if, though new to the district, she already knew who Garret was. I held up my hand.

"She's not bad," my friend said. "You should hit that."

"A kid just died," I said.

Garret shrugged, rounded his finger in the air. "Circle of life." Then: "Heads-up, she's coming over. Looks like she's gonna try and shoot her shot."

I looked. She was, indeed, navigating between the tables and chairs and heading our way.

"Well," I said. I pushed my glass back and forth between my fingers.

"Hi," she said.

"Hello," Garret responded.

"I'm sorry, could I—" she touched the back of a chair and looked across the table at me. "I was wondering if I could ask you some questions? About our department?"

Before I could answer, an abrupt sound—a burst of air escaping from behind Davis's larynx—startled us all. His head rose partway up out of the wreckage of his arms, then returned to the table.

Garret stood up. "I'm gonna mosey," he said.

I rose, too, and offered my hand across the table. "I'm William. Mr. Able."

"Lauren," she said. "Ms. West."

Under normal circumstances, the beginning of the school year six full weeks behind us in August, these introductions might have already taken place, but the high school's English department and the district's administration hadn't been getting along for the last three or four semesters—had been at war, really—and before this year's first department meeting the veteran teachers in my department had been warned against speaking with the incoming new teachers. At that meeting our first-years had been chaperoned in by a trio of the principals from math, science, and social studies, and the annual "stand up and introduce yourself" portion of the meeting had been omitted. I had only seen Lauren West a few times since, and we had never spoken.

She gestured toward the loosened tie I was still wearing from the day's memorial services. "I didn't know him. Did you have him in class?" *Him* was Bryce. Half the people at the bar had been at the funeral, and the whole school had been in mourning for a week.

"As a junior," I said. "But I met him when he was eight." I nodded toward Davis. "That's his older brother."

A look of misgiving overtook Lauren's face. "I'm so sorry. Should I—"

I shrugged away her concern. "It's fine. I answer questions for a living. What do you want to know?"

She shook her head. "No—"

Having been a first-year teacher myself only three years before—and having taken part in other conversations with other first-years several times since—I felt I might be able to intuit the nature of her questions. "It's not the kids," I said. "The kids are just kids. You can't blame them. And it's not their parents. A lot of them are actually pretty good, or can't help being bad. It's the admins. The admins and the legislators."

Lauren started to stand. "Maybe I—"

"No, hold on." I motioned for her to sit back down. I'd spent the morning at the church and the rest of the day at Davis's parents' house while his mother had worn a brittle smile and Davis and his father and several of their near and distant relations had drunken themselves to numbness and obliteration. The opportunity to dish on the awfulness of the school Lauren and I both worked at now rose up as a welcome reprieve. "It's a terrible place," I said. "It's where educational dreams go to die. You shouldn't stick around if you can help it. You should just put in your

two or three years and move on to get a better job somewhere else." This was typically what promising young
teachers from out of town did when they moved to Plains
City: earned enough experience to not be a 'new' teacher
anymore, then moved on to better paying jobs elsewhere
in suburbs where the kids were easier to work with.
Though I'd only glimpsed her a handful of times, it
seemed to me that Lauren West was a promising young
teacher in this mold.

Her eyes steadied on me. "Are you planning to go somewhere else?"

"This is my last year. After this I'm going to grad school,
or law school, maybe. I haven't decided."

Her brow creased and I saw the beginnings of a
teacherly scowl. She put her hands down on the table and
began to push herself up. "I can see that you're... bereaved.
I'll let you—"

"Hold up." I pointed to Davis, whose shoulders were
now rising and falling in steady rhythm. "Do me a favor and
sit with this guy. Just for a minute. I'll come back and talk to
you. Two minutes. I can tell you what you need to know."

She looked dubiously from me to Davis, then back to
me. She lowered herself back down to the table. "I'll be right
back," I said. "Promise."

A Chicano rap song was finishing as I moved off into the
bar. It ended, and in his booth, DJ Saucedo put on an old
George Strait ballad, causing a tidal shift in the comings and
goings on the dance floor. I was caught in the flow of the
younger and more ethnically rich group flowing out, then
brought up short by a button-hooking finger at the
vanguard of the denim-clad crowd flowing in.

"You're..." the pointing woman in front of me said, but
she couldn't seem to place me.

I searched her face. "Your daughter's teacher," I said at last. "Adrienne."

"My daughter's teacher," she said, snapping her fingers as if she had arrived at the conclusion on her own. She turned to address the man—big, burly, mustachioed—who, his hands on her hips, held her up marionette-style from behind. "This is Mr..."

"Able," I supplied.

"Mr. Able." Her smile was radiant. "He's Adrienne's..."

"English teacher."

Adrienne's mother—Ms. Gallegos—stared at me for a four- or five-count, then nodded and repeated my last two words. She twisted back to face her handler. "See how young he is? Adrienne loves him." She maneuvered back around to stage-whisper this piece of intelligence to me. "Adrienne *loves* you. And *I* would never miss your class." She reached up to pat my cheek.

I never knew how to respond to compliments like these. "I appreciate that," I said.

"Let's go," her handler said, hauling her back in. Her shirt rose as he hefted her, high enough to expose her midsection and one pink, satiny cup of her bra. His hand roved in for a squeeze as they passed, and I remembered Adrienne's beginning-of-the-year essay on the topic of adversity: how she had written about her parents' divorce and her experience watching her mother try to pass herself off as a teenager with a series of men Adrienne described variously as "old bums, pervs, and freaks." Then they were passed.

I acknowledged a number of acquaintances who propriety required me to acknowledge along the next twenty-yard stretch of my journey, a few friends of my parents' and a number of peers and colleagues closer to my own age, and then at the bar I saw and pretended not to see Jim Morris, Jr, the most junior partner at the downtown law firm that bore his surname twice and my own only once: Morris, Able, & Morris. But my pretending came to no avail —he had seen me, and called out, "Will, come grab a drink, man!" He held aloft his glass and indicated the open seat beside his own.

That there should be an open seat beside him on a night as busy as this one was a fact that spoke for itself. I shook my head and pointed to the bathroom, holding up my wrist and pointing my thumb over my shoulder to supply the rest of what he needed to know.

He grinned wolfishly, reading more into my gesturing than there was to read. "Git 'er done," he called to me. "Another time."

Lauren West didn't look pleased when I arrived back at the table where my friend had passed out. "Did you want to —" I started to ask.

"The students don't have anywhere to go," she said.

"I'm sorry?"

"You said I should put in my two or three years and leave. That's not fair to the kids. They can't just get up and go."

My first impulse was to argue: the students certainly *could* go if they wanted. They could go by *graduating*, as many did, or go by *dropping out*, as did many others. But I checked this impulse. Lauren was gathering herself, getting ready to leave. It occurred to me she was still new and idealistic. A person who had, presumably, grown up *wanting* to teach. She had been cut off from the veteran teachers in our department by the draconian actions of our administration and was uninitiated and untutored, as of yet, in the bleak and mordant ways teachers regularly spoke to one another when students weren't around. I held up my hands and motioned for her to stay.

"You're right," I said. "I'm bereaved. And I'm tired. And some of what I said was gallows humor." I tried to smile. "You said you had a question. Some questions. Ask me. Let me try to help."

She looked as if she knew that doing so was a bad idea, and then sat back down anyway. "It's about the 'no books' thing."

"That's a good question to ask."

"We're not allowed to teach them?"

"We're not supposed to."

"But some people do?"

"It's kind of a form of... nonviolent resistance. The district doesn't want us to teach some things, and sometimes we teach those things anyway."

She looked at me skeptically. "At the beginning of the year, we new teachers were told that we were only supposed to teach district-approved and district-supplied materials, and that if we didn't we could get fired."

"Yes," I agreed. "That's accurate."

"And that they fired people last year for teaching material—books—that they weren't supposed to teach."

"Elizabeth Gray and Sarah Teller. Both first-years. They were non-renewed."

"So *first-year* teachers can't teach books, but more established and tenured teachers can?"

I shook my head. "They can fire tenured teachers. It's just more difficult. They have to go through due process."

"And you're tenured?"

I shook my head again. "I'm starting my fourth year. You have to have finished four to be tenured."

"But I hear *you're* teaching material from the off-curriculum list. Trickster tales to you juniors? And some of Chaucer to your seniors? And I heard Mrs. Rosenbaum and Mrs. Dennison teach *a lot* of material from off-curriculum. And Valerie Stephens, too. They're teaching *A Midsummer Night's Dream* and Emily Dickinson and *I Know Why the Caged Bird Sings*."

Lauren West was like an honors student who'd been misplaced in a regular class. I could answer her questions, but it was hard to know where to start. "It's kind of complicated..." I began.

"I'm not a stupid person."

"I'm just trying to think how to explain. Part of it is that some of the veteran teachers are kind of... grandfathered in. We were teaching the old curriculum when the new one was introduced, and there were some agreements about a transitional period."

By the expression on her face, I could tell that she didn't find this answer either sufficient or fair.

"And part of it has to do with history. Mrs. Rosenbaum and Mrs. Dennison have been in the building a long time. Parents in the community like them. Their oldest kids had them, and they want their younger ones to have them, too. They've been named Teachers of the Year."

"That doesn't account for you and Ms. Stephens."

"Valerie and I get students to pass the test. If the admins get rid of us, they run the risk of replacing us with teachers who can't get kids to pass."

This seemed to compute for Lauren West, if only grudgingly. "So if I fall in line and get my kids to pass the state tests this spring, then maybe I can teach real books next year?"

I winced. "I'm not sure that's exactly the case."

"Where do you guys get the books? They told us there aren't any in the building."

"We have a big closet's worth. It's by the stairs in the English wing."

"And they don't lock it?"

I dug in my pocket and pulled out my keyring. "Some of us have keys. We go in after school when no one is around."

"Where'd you get the—"

"The janitors." I grinned at the memory. "We just told them we needed new copies a few weeks after the admins changed the locks the last time."

"So if I wanted a set of books, you could get me one?"

"Or you could just ask a janitor. Most of them will let you in."

I peered down at what was left in the bottom of my glass, tried to decide if I wanted another drink or not. A weight came down on my shoulder, and when I looked up, Adrienne Gallegos's mother was teetering above me. Beer sloshed from the bottle in her hand, landing in my lap, and when she spoke, it was in the manner of a sports fan calling from ten yards away instead of a parent standing with her hand on my shoulder. "I'll tell Adrienne I saw you. There's nobody like you, Mr. Able!"

Her handler grunted his own sentiment and reeled Adrienne's mother back in. Lauren West cocked an eye at me. "Former student?"

"Mother of a current. Having a hard time of it."

She nodded and a moment passed. Davis surprised us with another of his abrupt snores.

"What was he like?"

I looked at my slumbering friend. "Davis? He's a good guy. Played football, has a degree in business—"

Lauren shook her head. "The brother. The kid who... is no longer with us."

Even if Davis was out cold, I could never speak freely about Bryce with him so near. "He was really special. Kind of important." The words stung for their truth and insufficiency, and my vision began to blur. I decided against another drink. I was ready to be done for the night. "Do you want to go see it? The spot?"

"The spot?"

"The spot where he rolled. It's a couple miles from here. We could drive."

She drew back at this suggestion, and her expression, which had been sympathetic a moment before, shifted to something harder and disapproving. "We work together. Nothing romantic is going to happen between us."

"I didn't think it was," I said, recognizing how false I might sound. "I just thought you might want to see it. I drive out there a lot. Every night."

She scrutinized me, as if trying to discern whether or not I was an honest person, and I tipped back like a student in my chair to show my indifference to her judgement. "You're right, I'm in mourning," I said when she didn't seem to reach any conclusion. I tipped back forward. "You should get out of here. Go see your friends." I stood and nodded across the bar. Then, abruptly feeling I'd perhaps been too callous, I leaned forward. "You can come by my room at the school anytime. I know what it's like to be a new teacher, and that it's not an easy building to find help in. I can help you if you need it. I need to get out of here now, though."

She looked as if she might say something else, then— offer an argument or defense or some criticism—but a glance at Davis seemed to persuade her now wasn't the time or place. "I'm sorry about your friend's brother," she said, and she stood and walked back across the bar.

Garret said he could get Davis home, and I paid my tab and left the Oasis ten minutes later, finding myself in the wind-blown warmth of a late-September night. My car was parked in one of the front rows of the lot; I backed it out and drove it the four blocks to the familiar stoplight on Main where a right turn would get me home to my building and a left would carry me out over the train tracks, across the bridge, and to River Road, the two-lane stretch of asphalt running parallel to the Arkansas I had already driven perhaps twelve hundred times in my life. I turned left, and the streetlights thinned out and the glow of the stars brightened as the city receded behind me. A couple miles down River Road I encountered a line of old cars and caught sight of a low yellow glow: the dying light of a high school river party at one of the half-dozen flat places where the kids, as I and my friends had when we were students, had stolen a truckload of wooden pallets from behind the local Kroger to light a bonfire for a river party. I slowed as I passed, saw a dozen or so kids celebrating after the midnight curfew and risking trouble when the sheriffs made their rounds. The spot I was looking for was another half-mile along, at a banked turn. I pulled over onto the side of the road when I reached it, got out, and found the ruts.

Davis and I hadn't become friends until we were juniors at PCHS. Members of two rival friend groups from the two rival middle schools in town, our separate groups had come together that fall to pull a prank on the Thursday night eve of a more important rivalry—our football team's rivalry with the Dodge City Red Demons, an hour's drive to the east. We had decorated a trio of eight-by-ten particle boards with some choice obscene slogans, packed a few cans of spray paint in case we should find occasion to use them, and purchased a number of cheap, frilly women's undergarments to decorate some of the well-known cowboy statues near the DCHS stadium. We'd done our painting on a slab of concrete in Davis's back yard, and departed in our short caravan of second-hand Fords and Chevys a little after nine o'clock. It was after midnight when we returned; the raid was a rousing success. Since the next morning was a day off of school—there were fall inservice meetings for teacher—we'd celebrated in Davis's basement with a couple of cases of Coors and a pint of peppermint schnapps. When I awoke on the couch in front of the TV there the next morning, I found eight-year-old Bryce sitting beside me playing Goldeneye on the Nintendo 64.

Davis and I became better friends in the years that followed—we ultimately roomed together in the dorms as freshmen and shared a house for three years while we earned our degrees—and so it was fair for him to think I had attended the funeral in support of him. But Bryce had been almost like a brother to me, too—I hadn't had my own little brother—and Bryce had been my *student*, one of my first, maybe my most important. I owed him, in a way I couldn't have explained to his brother or Lauren West, a complex debt of gratitude. Because the second-grade kid I had hoisted on my shoulders in the stands at that Friday night's game against Dodge City my junior year, the kid I taught a shot fake with a basketball in his driveway, had grown to be *big*, a man-sized junior with facial hair like his brother who could, like his brother, buy alcohol at the Vietnamese liquor store on 4th Street. *Bigger* than Davis had been in high school, even, and Davis had been enormous, an all-conference linebacker before Bryce had made his way to being all-state.

While I knew him and knew that he wasn't *mean*, Bryce often came across that way, and could clearly be... aggressive. He had a mouth that, as his father and mother's son—and as Davis's little brother—largely ran unfiltered. A student in Mr. Charter's Junior English class during my first year in the building, he had taken umbrage at a few assertions the 60-year-old man had made about Bryce's performance in the classroom and fired back a number of expletives in return, punctuating his thoughts with a thrown copy of the book they were reading that struck Mr. Charter's head, resulting in an injury that took the man out of the building for two days and required, on the superficial level of his scalp, six stitches.

As major an infraction as it was, it was technically his first, and Bryce was, as a junior, already an integral part of the school football team's defensive unit. He took a two-day suspension from class, rode the bench for the first half of the game that Friday night, and was switched out of Mr. Charter's English class to be placed in my own.

This was a coincidence.

The counselors, I don't think, had any knowledge of my previous relationship with Bryce Davis. They had put him into my room because there had been no other open section of junior English that hour, and emailed to let me know it was happening the morning before he showed up. The class was tough. A "low" section loaded with known behavior-issue juniors and students on the principals' "graduation watch list." A few of the boys—jocks, wannabes, and would-be gangsters—made some noise when Bryce walked in, and Stephani Campbell, a held-back senior wearing a court-assigned electronic ankle bracelet, raised her eyes to meet his as if the two might have had some history, or perhaps future. The bell rang, the class's volume rose. "This ought to be good," I heard one of my worst-offenders say.

I said "Good morning," and none of my students quieted or said anything to me in response. Then I said—I don't remember what I said. Something that was clearly inadequate and ineffectual. The kid who had thought things *ought to be good* leaned forward to swipe Bryce's elbow and get his attention, and I watched Bryce's face turn red as he tore his arm away. Bryce brought both of his hands down on the top of his desk, and, in a moment, had everyone in the room's attention in a way I, in the course of the semester, had never had. "Everybody *shut up*," he said. "Mr. Able is trying to *teach*."

The class quieted down.

So it was that Bryce Davis, penetrator of opposing lines, ransacker of backfields, flattener of quarterbacks, and bane of offensive coordinators across the region, became, in my classroom, not only my unbidden enforcer, but also my biggest cheerleader and best student. When I read passages out loud, Bryce clapped his hands and hollered for me to read more. When I lectured, he sat up straight on the edge of his seat and took notes. When he left, he called out "Thanks Mr. A" and took to high-fiving and fist-bumping me on his way out. Over the course of the next month, most of the other boys, and some of the girls—even Stephani Campbell—took to doing the same.

By the end of the semester, I had developed a reputation. I could appeal to and reach jocks in the same way Ms. Stephens appealed to our musical and artistic students, the way Mrs. Dennison reached the English as a Second Language students, and Mrs. Rosenbaum inspired our most high-flying gifted and honors students. And I wasn't bad with the angry or disaffected kids at the school, either.

Leaning into my new reputation, I made analogies comparing long passages to "easy weights" and short, dense texts to "heavy lifting." I taught some "tough guy" poetry, and when it came time to write in class, employed a stopwatch, exhorting my students to exceed their personal bests of one paragraph, half a page, a page and a half. I wasn't like one of those movie teachers—I wasn't staying long hours after school, taking kids under my wing to tutor them, or crying when they failed. And certainly the behavior improvements were incremental, the reading still faulty, the writing still filled with basic grammar, capitalization, and spelling errors. But I was running my class, and kids were learning. At the semester break a number of coach Stuckey's varsity baseball players and coach Arroyo's wrestlers were transferred into my sections. The next fall I was assigned all of the football team's junior starters and both co-captains of the volleyball team.

Bryce had paid attention in my class—he had paid attention to *me*. I had said things and he'd valued them—*accepted* them—because I had said them, because they were important to *me*. I wondered now, not for the first time standing beside Old River Road in the last week, if there was anything I could have done that might have saved his life: offered some other lesson, assigned him a key text. If he'd had me as his teacher senior year instead of Mrs. Dennison, might he have become less reckless, more prudent? Might he have lived?

But it was almost certainly a mistake to attribute myself so much influence. My stronger sense was that my ability to effect positive change in his life had hit its limit; that he was an 18-year-old kid growing up and playing football in Plains City, Kansas, his father and mother's son, Davis's little brother, product of Plains City, America in the late 20th and early 21st century. If any of my lessons, or Mr. Charter's, or Mrs. Dennison's had had any real impact, they wouldn't have been felt until after at least a few years had passed, after some of that thick skin of adolescent rage and defiance had been sloughed off.

I bent to pick up and handle a shard of broken plastic the color of his truck's blue body. The night was cooling and I smelled wood fire on the breeze. By the alchemy of some physical and psychic transubstantiation, I recalled one of my own high-speed trips down the road behind me that Bryce had so recently departed: Garret, a cheerleader named Krista Lacy, and me getting Krista's black Nissan Maxima up to a hundred and twelve miles an hour on a Thursday night after a week of working on a US history presentation together, Krista holding the wheel steady and braking expertly despite the half-bottle of strawberry Boone's Farm she'd downed.

I walked further away from the road, down a narrow trail through the waist-high sagebrush into the sandier soil at the riverbed's edge, where I was visited by another memory, this one from the honors section of English II I had been enrolled in during my own junior year: Mrs. Unger reciting Langston Hughes's "The Negro Speaks of Rivers" to my class from the front of the room while my peers and I followed along in our books. The effortless rhythm of the words; the way this river-poem had felt ocean-deep. Soul-deep. After she had finished her reading, Mrs. Unger had turned to draw a picture of a forking river on the board, populating its banks with simple illustrations of people, animals, docks, and houses. She had explained that *We not only live* by *rivers,* but *We live by rivers.*

In his poem, Hughes wrote of the Euphrates, the Congo, the Nile, and the Mississippi, the massive waterways of our world, the watery roads of human history. Not for the first time standing at my own riverbed's edge, I tried to imagine them: the Nile feeding the aqueducts of the pharaohs, the Congo pulsing like an artery from deep in the heart of Africa. In the deep blue of my western Kansas night, I thought about the Mississippi, especially, that longest, broadest river in the country where I lived. The river Twain had written about. What relation could it or these other rivers have to me, Bryce, my current students, or the river we knew? What commonality could be shared in the tributaries of these branching family trees?

I stepped down into the soft, sandy bottom of the Arkansas. In his poem, Hughes suggested a connection between river-depth and soul-depth. What depth could my soul have? How deep could the souls of my people be? On the western half of Kansas, the Arkansas was dry.

2

The truth of the matter was that I never planned to teach, never wanted to be a teacher. Not that I hadn't liked school, or been good at it. I had; I was. But the profession never held an allure for me as it does for some. Not once did I ever look at one of my own teachers and think *Yes. That. I would like to do what he* (or more likely *she*) *does for a living.* To the contrary, if someone had told me when I was a 17- or 18-year-old that I would grow up to head a classroom, I'd have likely read an implied insult in the statement. My earliest understandings of teachers came from my father, of Morris, Able, & Morris fame, the school district's chief legal counselor. The "those-who-can'ts" he called them, and "school marms," "babysitters," and "mother hens." His most withering appellations were reserved for the men in the profession. "The eunuchs," he called them. Trent Richards, the head of the Social Studies department and longtime head of the Teachers' Union, with whom my father annually negotiated contracts, he referred to as "the Eunuch in Chief." (As legal counsel, my father occasionally took up cases on behalf of teachers for the school district, but more often than not he acted on the side of the school board and administrators against the staff.) And so I had *liked* some of my teachers, and even *admired* some of them. Many, in fact. But to *be* a teacher, I understood, was to pursue the lowest of the professions a person with professional ambitions might pursue. Not something I was interested in.

If the twin shames of my life at the age of twenty-five, then, were 1) the fact that I had returned to my hometown after college, and 2) become a teacher, then the place I found refuge from my humiliation was the apartment I rented in the Douglas Building above Main Street, downtown. Once a hotel, then an agricultural office building, now converted to a number of hastily divided and rough-hewn apartment living spaces, I lived in a three-room space on the fourth floor there: a small bedroom, small living room, and small office, laid out train car-style along a narrow interior hallway that ran parallel to the cigarette smoke-filled hallway outside my door. My apartment featured close proximity to the building's laundry room just down the hall, an elevator at my end of the building, and the oft-used back staircase, also at my end of the building. While these amenities were nice, the feature that most sold me on the place was the view it offered from its western-facing windows. Looking out over the tops of the Wendell and the Riley buildings across the street in the foreground, these views reminded me of big city life as depicted on television sitcoms and in Hopper paintings: "Night Windows," or "Room in Brooklyn." In the distance, on the other side of the railroad tracks and the empty riverbed, I could see the grasses of the High Plains moving sea-like on a windy day, and could watch far-off thunderheads gather and sheets of rain sweep across the prairie when it stormed. On a hot, still, clear afternoon in the summer, I could almost see—almost imagine I saw—a ghost outline of the far-off Rockies.

Which is all to say that in my apartment on the fourth floor of the Douglas Building, I was both aloft from Plains City and aloof from it, too. I slept in on the Sunday morning after the funeral, picking up my coffee and a breakfast sandwich at Wonder's Bakery on my building's first floor when it opened at ten o'clock, and I read and watched television by turns throughout the late morning and afternoon as my air conditioner cycled on and back off. I stepped out again a little after five to pick-up takeout at Dos Amigos across the street, and came back upstairs to eat it on my couch, my worn, clothbound Webster's Collegiate dictionary serving as a makeshift TV tray while I watched a popular high fantasy movie I had received in a red envelope in my mailbox. Then I finished the evening on my couch reading more of my book and watching an episode of *Cheers* and an episode of *Frasier* before turning in around eleven. It was a day in which I had only spoken to two other people and probably shared less than thirty words between the two; no wizard self-exiled in his tower could have passed a day more contentedly.

But then when I woke it was Monday, time to shave, shower, dress, and descend the Douglas building's back staircase, a descent that meant coming down in more ways than one. I was never so miserable as on the Monday mornings I drove the eight blocks down Main Street to the high school I had once graduated from, feeling lower and lower at each of the stoplights that I had to stop at along the way, leaving my elevated life behind.

If I felt *low* on my drives to school, however, it was a

lowness I knew, after three years' experience, I wasn't destined to suffer long. Invariably, walking the halls and seeing the eagerness, awkwardness, and merriment of the students would lift my spirits—or seeing their torpor, misery, and loneliness would prompt me to dig deep and bring out a better version of myself for their benefit. This morning my turning-point came sooner than I expected. As soon as I stepped out of my car in the teachers' parking lot, I met the front end of a cadre of band students coming back in off the practice field after their zero-hour marching practice.

"Hey Able," a voice called. I turned and saw Dylan Bell, the captain of the drum line and an alumnus of my class. The white and silver snare drum strapped to his front glittered in the morning light.

"Morning Dylan," I called, and even as the words were flying my mouth, Dylan was *rat-a-tatting* and calling "Fall in!" to his charges. Then there was more *rat-a-tatting*, the sudden, twinned *ta-dump*s of the bass drums, and the wild pounding of the other drummers spinning up to their full feat of syncopated madness. I became, as I walked into the school with my satchel slung over my shoulder, a kind of Pied-Piper figure, the grinning head of a parade of irreverent band students returning to their lockers.

"Yo Mr. A, what'd you do this weekend?" Javier Galvon asked after the bell had rung to start my day's first class.

At the beginning of the year, I had tried shutting Javi down when he invariably launched off on one of these tangential discussions at the start of class, but the young man was irrepressible, a born talker with perhaps some undiagnosed ADHD. Trying to shut him down sometimes made him sullen and spiteful. And I had realized that his attempts at conversation weren't mean-spirited or particularly designed to drag the class off course; he was just being friendly and trying to connect. I'd found that if I humored him a little bit early in the day, I could often get him to work for me for the rest of the period. This morning the class was light by more than a half-dozen students, anyway. Talking to Javi for a few minutes might give some other kids time to show up. "Read books, mostly," I said. "Did you have a good weekend?"

Javi ignored my question. "Nuh-uhh," he said, stretching out the last syllable and pointing an accusatory finger at me. "I heard you hit the *club*."

In a town the size of Plains City, where there were really only so many places to go on the weekend, and where so many of the high school kids had older siblings and friends who either visited the Oasis regularly or worked there, there was little point in trying to guess where a junior football player like Javi Galvon might have heard about my weekend outing. "I did," I said. "I hopped on a private jet Friday after school and flew out to Miami. We were in the club all night. I saw Lebron and Kobe and that rapper you guys like. What's-his-name. Five Dimes."

"Who?"

"Give me a sec. Not Five Dimes." I shook my head, pretended to think. "Ten Nickels?"

Marcos Dominguez, Javi's closest friend from the football team, barked his short laugh. "He's talkin' Fiddy," he called. "Fiddy Cent."

I shook my head. "No, that doesn't sound right. Half-a-Buck. Is his name Half-a-Buck?"

Javi and several of my students groaned, a reaction I couldn't help but smile at.

"Hey, Able. Did you do some shots?" Raphael Lerma wanted to know. "Jaeger bombs and tequila?"

"*So* many shots," I said. I pinched a finger and thumb in front of my chin, extending my pinky. "But we weren't shooting Jaeger or tequila. It was espresso."

There were more groans.

"Espresso?" Raphael's look was disgusted.

"Lebron kept buying. When he's done with basketball, he told me his next dream is to get into the rap game. He wanted to talk about rhyme schemes and poetry. We both like Tupac."

"*Man*, I know you didn't—" Javi started, his voice going high, but I cut him off, pretending I had just remembered something else.

"Jay-Z was there! And Beyoncé! They didn't show up until pretty late, but they wanted to talk about poetry, too. We're thinking about collaborating. We wrote a bunch of stuff down on napkins." I patted my pockets, as if I might still have some of these notes with me. "It was lyrics for a song we're going to call..."

My students leaned in.

"'English Grammar!'"

They fell back. More groaning. This was enough for Javi. He threw his hand up in exasperation. "Man, I ain't even gonna play with you," he said. "Teach your class, man."

MY LESSON for the day was from the so-called 'old curriculum,' a traditional junior-level tour of American Literature. Having finished our beginning-of-year unit on Native American creation myths and trickster tales, and having moved through some writings of the first European explorers and colonizers, I was getting ready to start my unit on the Puritans, beginning with some old poems, sermons, and historical context before reading Arthur Miller's play *The Crucible*. Before I got that ball rolling, today I wanted to squeeze in a poem I had been thinking about over the weekend, which I had made copies of when I'd walked into the building. I was halfway finished passing my copies of it down my students' rows of desks when Mrs. Hirsche, the district's Head of Literacy, walked into the room. Austerity personified, Mrs. Hirsche was a former fourth- and fifth-grade teacher who had picked up a doctoral degree and joined the ranks of the administration several years before. She was wearing a white blouse, red jacket, black skirt and black stockings, and had on red lipstick and a not insignificant application of rouge. Affixed to the lapel of the jacket was the silver title badge worn by all of the Central Office staff: Janine Hirsche, Head of Literacy. She looked, perhaps more prominently than she ever had before to me, like the hope-crushing, nightmare-inspiring villain from one of the Disney movies of my youth. Cruella Deville, or the evil queen from *Snow White.*

Our eyes met for only the briefest of moments—*I'm here; I'm observing your class*, hers said—and, without apologizing for interrupting, without a friendly *nice to see you*, she stalked back to the back corner of the room to begin recording her observations of my teaching. As I watched the last of my dittoed copies move to the end of the last row of my students' desks, she began moving her pen, counting how many boys were in the room, how many girls, and what percentages of my students seemed to be white, black, Hispanic, and Asian for the 'demographics' portion of her walk-through form. Next she would circle descriptors of 'mood' and 'atmosphere,' then make a note of whether or not any of my students were violating dress code, and another as to whether or not *I* was professionally dressed before finally copying down the learning goals I had listed on the board for the day. It was a form all of the principals and some of the other district administrators from the Central Office carried around all day, popping into various classrooms to take their measurements. Some teachers, either as a show of courtesy, or to ensure that they received proper credit for everything they did, slowed down or even paused their teaching when administrators walked in, but I had become impatient with the four- and five-times-a-week interruptions of my class. I typically tried to keep teaching at the same pace I had been moving at before the admin walked in. Sometimes, out of spite, I moved faster.

Which isn't to say I didn't let the walkthroughs change my teaching. I did, and didn't know many teachers—besides Mrs. Rosenbaum or Mrs. Dennison, perhaps—who didn't. After taking her measurements and copying down my goals from the board, Mrs. Hirsche would begin checking off "high yield" teacherly strategies that I used. The district had measured an average of six "high yield" strategies being used during ten-minute walkthroughs the year before, and had made a goal of eight for this year. Teachers who earned more checkmarks typically saw less walkthroughs as the year progressed; teachers who earned fewer saw more. My average, according to Mr. Avery, the English Department principal, was eleven and a half, though once I had hit nineteen.

As she finished taking her initial notes and looked up, I walked down one of the aisles between my students' desks to the back corner of the room opposite Mrs. Hirsche, then walked back to the front along a different one. *Teacher makes use of proximity to regulate student behaviors: check.*

"Alright," I said. "We're going to read a poem by a poet name Octavio Paz. Before we get started, I want to take care of a little vocab work on the board, so if you guys would go ahead and get out your notebooks..." I paused and waited for my students to retrieve their notebooks from their bags —an activity that took more time than I might have preferred—then went on, uncapping a marker and writing on the board as I did so. "We'll start with three vocab words: 'monosyllable,' 'perpetual,' and 'syllogism.'" *Instructor provides context and background: check. Instructor guides student notetaking: check. Instructor teaches vocabulary: check.*

I went through the definitions of the words, providing a few examples of monosyllable words and several of syllo-gisms (*Instructor teaches by example and/or analogy: check*), asked the students to read silently (*Students practice silent reading: check*) and then called on Adrienne Gallegos to read the poem out loud to the class (*Students read aloud: check*). When she was finished, *I* read the poem aloud, and then, when I was finished, I asked if there were any questions (*Instructor checks for understanding: check*). There weren't, and I told my students to pick up their pencils. "We're going to do some basic annotation," I said, and guided them through a quick round of mark-ups (*Students annotate texts: check*) and told them to tear out a sheet of paper. "We're going to write about the poem," I said. "About a half-a-page. Four questions. What is the situation of the poem? Where does the poem 'turn,' or 'shift'? Why is the poem called 'After'? And what is the poem about—that is, what does it *mean*?" I wrote these questions on the board. (*Instructor provides both verbal and written questions: check. Students write: check.*)

Mrs. Hirsche tucked her clipboard under her arm and let herself out of the classroom.

"Yo, who is that lady," Javi asked, scowling after the clicking of her heels had receded down the hall.

"That's Mrs. Hirsche," I said. "Don't worry. She's here to watch me, not you."

His scowl softened to a look of sympathy. "Sorry bro," he said. "She looks like a hater."

3

I didn't have to wait long after Mrs. Hirsche's walkthrough for the email inviting me to the principals' conference room. It showed up fifteen minutes after she had gone, giving me the rest of my first block and all of my second to wonder what fate I might have in store. Having led my first block through a discussion over the Paz poem, given them some notes over the Puritans, and guided them through a couple of Anne Bradstreet poems, I washed, rinsed, and repeated my lessons with my second group of students, then waited for a few minutes after the passing bell had rung before departing for the office. In the principals' conference room I found, to my surprise but not necessarily relief, that it was only Mrs. Hirsche waiting to speak with me. None of the principals were present.

"You're having quite the semester," she said after I'd taken my seat. I saw that she had not one, but perhaps fifteen or twenty walkthrough forms fanned out before her on the conference room's table. Every walkthrough that every administrator had done in my room so far this semester, I supposed.

"I've been teaching," I agreed.

She clucked her tongue, as if to suggest mine was an opinion we might not share. "Before we get into the class I saw today, let's talk about a few of these other forms I've had a chance to look over, shall we?"

I agreed that we should.

She slid out the first four or five forms from the fan. "It looks like you're still teaching a beginning of year grammar unit, and that you've had your students write..." she leaned forward. "You call them 'position papers,' and that you're still teaching the outdated curriculum to all of your junior level test-prep classes."

"I'm teaching a modified version of the old curriculum," I said, to get it on the record. "I've worked more test-prep materials into it. I like it for the sense of continuity—"

Mrs. Hirsche shook her head. "But we removed the old curriculum eighteen months ago."

"And agreed to a transition period to move from the old one to the new. You said two years."

"I said it *might* take two years. But we've completed the transition, and the expectation we laid out at the beginning of *this* school year was that teachers meet the requirements of the *new* curriculum. The new curriculum's focus is the test-prep standards."

I nodded and leaned forward, pointing to the space at the top of the first form she had in front of her. "I've bunked the standards from the new curriculum in with the materials from the old one. That should be documented. I was trying for a kind of 'best of both worlds' approach, and we've been using context clues, making inferences, drawing conclusions, multiple choice—"

"Yes," she said, using both of her hands to further separate and point at the forms in front of her. "And you've been teaching persuasive writing, narrative writing, essay structure, poetic devices, theme—"

"Those are all listed standards in the state curriculum guides."

"But they're not the *isolated standards* we've chosen to focus on in *our* curriculum, and they're not the standards we have listed in *these portions* of our curriculum guides."

"But if the students are going to do well on their annual persuasive writing assessments," I suggested, employing an argument I had heard Mrs. Rosenbaum and Mrs. Dennison employ successfully two years before.

"But the district is no longer *conducting* a persuasive writing assessment, Mr. Able."

I feigned ignorance of this point. "Is that decided? I thought that was just last spring, in light of last year's emergency situation."

"Last year's emergency situation has become *this* year's situation."

I held up my hands in *mea culpa* fashion. "I'm sorry. I've been operating under the assumption that we're still supposed to teach students how to write. If that's not the case anymore, I can adjust my teaching."

Her eyes narrowed. "I don't think you're being entirely sincere. We took writing out of the curriculum three semesters ago. The district changed the curriculum at the beginning of *last* year. We've talked to you and the members of your department about these changes at meeting after meeting for the last fifteen months, and you—" she spread her hands out over the walkthrough forms, which I now saw probably numbered closer to thirty-five or forty than fifteen or twenty —"haven't changed your instruction an iota or a jot."

I opened my mouth to defend myself, but no words

came. My breath caught. Perhaps sensing my vulnerability, Mrs. Hirsche pressed forward to take the ground I was ceding her.

"I have evidence of you teaching novels, plays, poems, literary movements and papers, but not once—*not once*—do I have evidence of you making use of district provided test prep materials."

"The materials aren't very good."

"The materials are aligned to the state tests."

"The kids don't respond to the materials. They hate them."

"We have absolutely *no* record of you teaching multiple-choice test-prep strategies—"

"I taught them. You guys didn't come in."

"And you've been getting materials from the off-curriculum list from the book room to teach your students. Against district policy. *Gatsby*, *Of Mice and Men*, and *Death of a Salesman* last semester."

"I wasn't planning to teach those again this year," I lied. "And *Death of a Salesman* is in the textbook. You said we could use materials from the textbook."

"We said you could use *short* materials from the textbook. We explicitly forbade *Death of a Salesman*. Last week you started the old curriculum's 'Rhetoric of the Revolutionary War' unit with your honors section. It doesn't seem like you're making any effort to change at all. Do you have anything to say about this?"

"That I regret having but one life to give for my country?"

Mrs. Hirsche sat back in her chair and sighed. "We were willing to look the other way during the transition to the new curriculum, Mr. Able, but the transition is over. We won't be doing so anymore. What would you say if I threatened to fire you?"

"That you might be doing me a favor?"

She nodded, as if this was what she had expected to hear. "We might do you that favor. I'm writing you up. You'll have a Form-57 in your file in the personnel office tomorrow." She stood and began to shuffle her papers together. "Oh," she said, looking at the one on top. "I'd meant to ask. Why were you teaching the Paz poem today? It wasn't in the old curriculum."

I looked at her. The answer, having to do with both Bryce's death and Adrienne Gallegos's mother, was complicated. Even if I *could* explain it succinctly, the Head of Literacy wouldn't want to hear it. "Context clues, inferences, and supporting details," I said. "They're all top-ten tested standards."

I CHECKED my phone after school and found a message from my father's secretary: "Hi William, it's Jean. Mr. Able would like to know if you're still available for dinner this evening, and we'd appreciate your calling back at your earliest convenience to either confirm or reschedule. You can reach me at..."

Per our existing arrangement, I called his secretary back, not him, to confirm that I was still free that night to have dinner with my father. "Great," she said amiably, and I heard her shift the phone to make a note with her pencil. "He'll see you at seven."

It was just shy of four. A new, cold wind was driving in from the north as I left the school, permeated with a heavy odor of feedlot. I drove home and tidied my apartment, took out the trash, and sat down on my couch to read until our appointed meeting time.

Though I remembered my father often saying critical things about other adults during my childhood, as if the adult world was full of people who were incompetent, my memories of his treatment of me were almost uniformly positive. He held me to a high standard, but had been a supportive and affectionate dad, teaching me to swim and shoot a basketball, challenging me with riddles and logic puzzles, never failing to make it to any of my little league games. It had been through various classmates and friends that I learned my father was feared in the town's legal community—that he was known to be exacting, and could be cruel. Our relationship had cooled when he and my mother divorced during my sophomore year of college, but that coolness, I think, was predominantly on my side of things. To his credit, he had done the majority of the work necessary to keep the lines of communication open between us. Perhaps because I hadn't wanted to disappoint him—or because I'd not wanted to incur his fabled wrath—I'd not told him about my decision to abandon my plans for law school and apply to graduate programs in English. I'd thought I would inform him of this from the relatively sure position of an acceptance: a TA-ship and a stipend. And then none of my graduate applications had panned out. Then I'd been finished with college, degree in hand, with credit card bills and my student loans about to come due, no prospects for a job or plans for the future in front of me. It was my father who had mentioned there were English positions open at the high school. Out of a desire to have me back home, I had thought at first, and out of a desire to scare me back towards applying to law school, I suspected later. And then one year turned into two, and two years became three. Now three had become four. Somewhere between the middle of my second year and the end of my third, the second or third time I told him I was putting off my law school plans again, the tone of our conversations began to change. I began to sense a chilliness from his quarter, as if my continuing to teach was a choice calculated to affront him. Now we had a more-or-less regular dining appointment once or twice a month, sometimes at his place at the country club, just as often at a restaurant in town. Tonight we were meeting at Kansas Pho Restaurant #1, just a couple blocks from my apartment, next door to his office.

As I passed the few hours before our dinner, I wondered, vaguely, if my father might have already heard about the Head of Literacy writing me up—which was ridiculous, of course. That paperwork wouldn't even be submitted yet, and would only go into my file in Human Resources. Mrs. Hirsche had idly *threatened* to fire me; my father wouldn't hear about such things unless the threat became a reality.

Arriving some ten minutes before our appointed meeting time, I wasn't surprised to find my father already seated in his customary booth, a seat that placed him, by my estimation, about fifteen yards from the chair he spent most of the rest of his day in. He was drinking an iced coffee— Thanh would sweep in and deposit one in front of me shortly after I was seated—and taking his 2nd or 3rd bite of one of the delicate, flaking egg rolls we would split the platter of. He looked at his watch when he saw me come in —one of his personal maxims was "if you're not early, you're late"—and I suspected I wasn't quite early enough to be on time. He stood to shake my hand when I approached. As the restaurant at this hour was about as dimly lit as he kept his office, the effect was of meeting him professionally across his desk.

"It's been too long," he said, more of an accusation than a formality—one that wasn't inaccurate. It had been almost two months since we'd seen each other last.

"The beginning of the school year," I said by way of explanation. He grunted, and I could tell this wasn't a path to go down. "How's Sharon?"

Sharon Rhodes was one of my father's many former secretaries from several cycles back—mother, coincidentally, to one of my former students, Bethany Rhodes, from my second year of teaching. Walking in through his open garage door an hour early for our last planned dinner of the summer, my call of greetings had precipitated her emergence from his master suite and into his living room wearing just two towels, one cinched around her waist, the other twisted atop her head. Her glasses resting on the suite's bathroom counter and my father and I's builds and voices being so alike, Sharon had been just two steps away from me, her arms spread wide, before I'd been able to convince her I wasn't my father.

"She's well."

"And you're—"

"I'm doing well."

A silence threatened to stretch out between us, but Thanh arrived with my anticipated drink. He and I had graduated in the same class at PCHS—had taken a number of classes together—and we always spent a grinning minute or so catching up—Thanh typically grinning more than me, I'm afraid. Then he took the same orders we always had ready without opening our menus.

"Do you remember Kelsey Pomerantz?" My father asked after Thanh had disappeared into the kitchen.

I had to think for a minute. "Bill Pomerantz's daughter? Jeff's little sister?" Bill Pomerantz was a newly-elected judge, his old law office formerly across the street from my father's. "Not really. Played tennis, maybe? I think she was three or four years behind me."

My father grunted again. "She's a year ahead of you now. She sent me a very nicely-phrased letter asking to clerk for me this summer."

I let the first half of this comment go. "You should take her on. Jeff was really good."

That Jeff, who had been valedictorian a year ahead of me, had already finished law school—and was doing quite well for himself in Kansas City—was a piece of recurring news my father had informed me of a few times over meals like this in the last three years.

"I think I will. I mention it because I suspect Bill would—"

"I know," I said, swallowing down about a quarter of an egg roll without having chewed it more than twice. "I'm sure he would."

During the quiet stretch that ensued, I resented my father for always taking the seat with the better view of the fish tank. Thanh showed up with our meals and we dug in, gradually transitioning into making the kinds of conversation that typified our dinners together—discussions of the weather, additions to and detractions from the local economy, and the KU men's basketball team's prospects for the upcoming season. At the conclusion of a monologue my father delivered on his thoughts about one of the Jayhawks' 4-star recruits, I found I wanted to talk about the trouble I had gotten into at the school earlier in the day. "What do you think about the high school's embargo against teaching books, anyway?" I asked.

He raised an eyebrow, a motion I took as his surprise I

would violate our tacit agreement against discussing district matters.

"If you'd rather not talk about your clients—"

"No. It's just I'm not sure I know what it is you're talking about."

I briefly sketched out the district's policy suspending the old, established curriculum and its longer written works to implement the new, short-passage and multiple-choice-focused one.

"The test-prep initiative." He shrugged. "Schools have to pass tests or risk their funding. I'm sure it's not so bad as you're suggesting."

"No, it is. No one's allowed to teach anything with any substance. I was written up this morning for teaching a poem in my class."

My father leaned back and finished chewing. "Was it an approved poem?"

"Should a poem need to be approved?"

"As I hear it, some of the instructors in your department aren't always teaching in the students' best interests."

"They've banned teaching *novels*," I said. "We're not allowed to teach Huck Finn or The Scarlet Letter."

My father looked as if he found this amusing. "Aren't those kind of passé in this day-and-age? How old is Huck now? A hundred and fifty? And you're not still making kids read Scarlet Letter, are you?"

I told my father that *Huck* was, indeed, about a hundred and fifty, and that two teachers had, until this year, been teaching it and *The Scarlet Letter* to their junior honors sections. "They're part of our heritage," I said. "Cultural touchstones." But my father still seemed indifferent. Unsure of how to press my argument, I reached for a pair of issues I knew him to care about. "It curtails teachers' first amendment rights. And not reading books flies in the face of the founding fathers' vision of a literate, educated society."

He lifted his napkin and laid it beside his plate. "I'm not sure freedom of speech supersedes a contractual obligation to follow a district-assigned curriculum. You seem awfully concerned for someone who isn't planning to be there a year from now."

I picked up my own napkin and folded it beside my own plate. "Maybe I should go into educational law," I said, reaching for my half-finished iced coffee. "Come back and sue the district for violating students' rights to a free and appropriate public education."

This, I was pleased to see, elicited a scowl. No mean feat, getting a visual reaction from Henry William Able. But as quickly as it had appeared, it was gone. In the next moment my father's face softened, and he picked up his own glass. "Maybe you will. It's always been one of my dreams to see you come back and practice law."

I circled the town on the bypass that Friday night, texting Garret from the long stoplight by the Route 50 Truck Stop to see about swinging by. *Door's open*, he texted back, so I switched on my turn signal and wheeled back into town.

Of the many ways Plains City is divided, one of the most easily recognizable is "the hill." More of a low plateau, really, the hill rises, zig-zag fashion, diagonally across the town, splitting it roughly between older and newer, poorer and richer, more darkly pigmented and more light. There are exceptions to this rule of the hill, of course. Older and more affluent neighborhoods exist at the lower elevation (where I, when my parents were still married, lived in my youth), and there are some more impoverished areas and poorly-built apartments up high. But the better elementary schools and real estate are generally understood to be "on the hill," and the lesser down low, and as Plains Citians talk, the rule generally abides. Garret's place was on the hill, at the less desirable end of a long, desirable street, in an unattractive little row of duplexes facing across to an as-yet undeveloped square of unkempt grass. Kemper's, an on-the-hill sports bar, was two-blocks away. I thought after meeting at his place he and I might head over to pass a couple hours there before I went home.

"Come on in, water's fine!" he called from his recliner as I let myself in the front door. He was typing something on his phone as he spoke and didn't look up at first. When he did, it was with a toothy grin. "Hot enough for ya? Grab a beer if'n you want one."

I did, and took a seat on his couch when I came back from his fridge. Watching him teach PE, coach baseball, go out to Kemper's or the Oasis a few times a week, and run through a revolving list of girls' numbers on his phone, I sometimes wondered why I couldn't simply adjust to life in Plains City like Garret. We watched a rerun Harrison Ford movie on his television until the first commercial break arrived, and then he looked across the room at me.

"You hear about the new teacher?"

"The math guy?"

Unable to control his students' behaviors, a first-year in the math department had simply walked out of his class-room the week before, driving his truck to the apartment he had rented at the beginning of August, packing up his things, and leaving town. His room had been without an instructor for the rest of the day, and none of the principals had known anything about it until he'd called the Central Office the next morning to resign.

"The math guy's old news. I'm talking about the gal in Science. The tiny one? On Wednesday."

I told him I hadn't heard.

"You know. She was from out of the country. From Malaysia or Polynesia or someplace. She called a group of pregnant girls in the back of her room a bunch of sluts."

"She said *sluts*? How many girls?"

He shrugged. Above him, the shadow thrown by the glow of his cell phone grew and receded on the ceiling as his hand moved back over it. "Two or three. Maybe four. It was a junior-level class, so there could've been any number. That's not the worst of it, though. Guess what she said when they tried to give her some lip?"

"No thank you? Quiet please?"

He shook his head. "Told them to shut up. To shut *the fuck* up."

"To shut the *fuck* up," I repeated.

He waved his hand. "Something like that. But she definitely dropped the f-bomb from what I heard."

"Do you think she knew? I mean, do you think she understood how inappropriate that was?"

His phone lit up, and he checked his message before turning back to face me. "See, that's the thing. I don't think anyone knows. English was like, either her second or third language, and who can tell if she gets our culture?"

I thought about how many times a person might hear the words 'slut' or 'fuck' walking through the lunchroom at PCHS. "She must've heard the kids say it all the time."

He finished typing another message and looked back up at me. "See, that's on the admins. You're going to go out of the country to hire teachers who don't speak English, you've gotta know you'll have to train them. Fuckers come in from places where the kids squat and write on chalkboards all day long. Where kids think it's a privilege to learn. How are they supposed to know what to do in an American class-room?" His phone lit up again.

"Who's that?" I asked.

He ignored my question and the commercial break ended. We watched another eight or ten minutes of the movie, and the next break came on. Garret looked down to check his phone, started typing. "Anything new going on with you?" he asked idly.

"I got written up this week."

He didn't look up. "Where'd you touch her?"

"I don't touch anyone anywhere but their minds and hearts. It was actually about this no books thing."

"Hmm," he said, fingers still moving.

"It's surprising, isn't it? I mean, it's books. I teach English. What would you do if they took away your basketballs and jump ropes?"

Garret only afforded this hypothetical a moment's consideration. "Run 'em more and do more push-ups. Not too hard to jump without a rope."

"It might not be quite so easy to stretch kids' brains as their muscles."

"Y'all in English might just not be as good of teachers as we are in PE."

"Don't you think it's at least pretty racist?"

The movie came back on. He shot me a glance. "Racist? I think you guys over in English are butt-hurt because they took away your toys. I read those books in school. Fuck if I know what good they did me."

"We're a minority-majority school and they're asking us to deliver an education that's less than the educations kids get in other schools in the state. Can you imagine what would happen if they tried to ban books in a majority white school on the east end of the state?"

"We're not teaching a bunch of white kids on the east side of the state. We're teaching a bunch of wetbacks out west."

I let the conversation go, stood to grab another beer from

his fridge. "You want to go to Kemper's after this," I asked when I got back.

He shook his head, lifted his phone. "I've got some action lined up."

"Is she legal?"

"Nope."

It was hard to tell whether he was serious or not. "Nobody I have in class, I hope."

"Don't get your panties in a bunch. She's twenty."

"Anybody I *had* in class?"

He shook his head. "She didn't have you. Her friend did. Want me to invite her?"

I said *No*, but Garret was already tapping on his phone.

"Her friend thought you were cute. You want me to try?"

I said *No* again, but he was still tapping. Looking back up, finally, he laughed.

"They're already feeling good," he said. "She's in."

I started to stand. "I don't think so."

"You don't even want to know who it is?" He pointed toward his kitchen. "I've got a case of beer in there that says the four of us could have a pretty good time."

I shook my head. "When're they going to get here? I'll clear out."

"'Bout half an hour. You used to be a lot more fun."

THE PARKING LOT behind the Douglas Building was full when I got home, and I could hear music echoing down from open windows on the top floor when I left my car in the lot across the street. A community college party.

I walked in through the building's rear entrance, called

the elevator, and stood beside the mailbox bank waiting for it
to come down. As it did, I heard two voices through its doors.
"—gonna fucking *do* something, though," said the first.

"He's a little bitch, anyway," said the other.

"Gonna fucking do some *shit*, though."

"Gabe, though—that guy's fucking crazy."

When the doors opened, I recognized the voices'
owners: Frank Weber and Eric Terriquez. I had seen the
former in my classroom some nine or ten hours before, and
would see the latter, if he ever chose to show back up, in my
fourth-hour class. Frank opened his mouth to talk, then
didn't. Eric just stood there.

"Weird, right?" I said. "You never know who you're going
to run into outside an elevator."

"Sorry Able," said Eric.

"Yeah, sorry," said the other.

Their backs to the wall, they slid out of the elevator, as if
giving me wide berth might keep me from smelling the
alcohol on their breaths and cigarette smoke on their
persons. And then they were out of the building, the glass
door swinging shut behind them.

"Be your best selves," I called after them, but I wasn't
sure if they could hear me. The elevator doors were already
closing, and then the cables and pulleys were carrying me
up to the fourth floor.

IN MY APARTMENT, the thumping of music and noise of
hallway footraces coming through the ceiling above me, the
recent events of the week shifted back and forth and became
muddled in my mind. I recognized that the thing to do was
take a shower, read a chapter of the book I was working on,

and go to bed. A night of sleep would do me good. I would be able to see things more clearly in the morning.

Walking into my room to retrieve my book from my nightstand, though, I was surprised to find my sheets and blanket missing. My immediate, ridiculous thought was of the community college students: that some of them had made rounds breaking into apartments in the building to steal people's bedclothes for some kind of impromptu toga party they must be having.

But my bedding was in the washer down the hall, of course. I had put it there after school as I did every Friday afternoon and then forgotten to move it to the dryer before driving over to Garret's. I had another set of sheets and another blanket, but the sheets were dirty, balled up at the bottom of my hamper. I couldn't use them unless they were both washed *and* dried. I would have to stretch the night out further, another forty-five or fifty minutes at least, reading in the laundry room as I waited on the dryer. Two more chapters of my book, then.

Leaving my apartment with a static sheet and handful of quarters, I found the hallway vacant, the laundry room unoccupied. I switched my load, pushed my dollar into the dryer's slots, and sat down in one of the chairs beside the folding table to start reading.

Try as I might, I couldn't involve myself in the book. I was in the last third of Conrad's *Lord Jim*, where the tone had shifted, and the events on Patusan, where the previously disgraced Jim became a kind of judicial guide to the native people, seemed too romantic and too far removed to follow naturally from the book's starting-out. Setting it down, I fell again to trying to sort out the events of my week. I thought of Mrs. Hirsche, my father, and Garret, and it occurred to me that my making any of them happy would result in my own being *un*happy; that I wasn't sure, at this particular juncture in my life, what I could do to make my own happiness come about. I was working over this dilemma when I sensed movement and was surprised by the appearance of Adrienne Gallegos in the laundry room's doorway.

"Fuck," she said.

I, too, was unsettled. Adrienne had a pink pass in one of her hands, and her sharp eyebrows were raised in alarm. For a moment, I didn't understand what she was doing in my building's laundry room so late at night, or why she should have a pink pass at all. Was she an office aide? Was I supposed to have a student with me who was now needed somewhere else, or did someone need me? Was Adrienne in the wrong place, or was I? And what was the protocol for correcting a swearing student aide who had brought a pink pass to the wrong room on a Friday night?

"Shit," she said as her mind caught up with the first word that had come out of her mouth. Her free hand came up and clamped itself over her lips.

My mind was catching up, too. As her empty hand rose, I saw that the flash of pink in her other wasn't a pass, but a Jack Daniels wine cooler. Adrienne wasn't in the room to find me or deliver a pass; she was out drinking with her friends at one of the parties upstairs and had had a bad time of it somehow. She had stumbled into the laundry room while looking for refuge. To run into me, her first-block English teacher, was mortifying: the shit-frosting atop the shit-cake of a hard night.

"I'm so sorry," she said, tears gathering on her lashes. "We do laundry for the bakery here. I thought—" but she couldn't tell me what it was she thought. Her face tied itself into a knot it would need time and several tearful spasms to untie itself from. "You can tell my mom," she said at last. "It's fine."

The memory of her mother swinging marionette-like in the arms of her mustachioed boyfriend the night of Bryce's funeral flashed across my mind. Would her mother even be sober enough to receive such a call this late on a Friday night? "If you need a ride, I think your mom would appreciate it more if the call came from you," I said. "Or maybe you have another safe ride?" I pointed at the bottle in her hand. "Somebody just handed that to you to hold onto for a second," I suggested. "You should probably throw it away." There was a trash can in the room, but it was beside me, and she didn't want to cross to my side of the room to get to it. This seemed wise. I didn't want her to cross to my side of the room, either. "Or you can just set it up there," I said, gesturing to the shelf above the coin exchanger beside the door.

Adrienne set the bottle there and, like a student with more questions to ask after the bell, lingered. She was a strong student, I reflected. Probably strong enough to be in an 'honors' section instead of my regular 'jock' one. Besides Adrienne, only two or three of the other students really seemed to have true academic interest. At once, I felt sorry I hadn't been able to elevate the level of discourse in our classroom for her, and resolved to make a recommendation to the counselors that she be placed in honors for her for senior year.

"Everyone who you don't think drinks really drinks all the time," she said. "Jenna Curtis is drunk upstairs. Elaina Delacruz is beyond gone."

Elaina Delacruz was the vice president of the senior class. "I don't know who Jenna Curtis is," I said.

"She's the sophomore on the cheerleading team. The littlest one."

The girl they threw into the air—the one from the top of the cheerleader's pyramids. Jenna was maybe five feet tall and probably weighed eighty-five pounds.

"Nick Hamilton smokes weed. Dwight Carroll and Keith Durham do too. They're all up there getting stoned."

I had Nick and Keith in class—neither of these facts surprised me. Nick's habit was probably innocent enough, but Keith might be on his way to bigger problems. "I don't know Dwight, either."

"He debates with Holly Steinmetz."

"Holly isn't up there, is she?" Holly Steinmetz was in one of Mrs. Rosenbaum's honors sections—she was one of the best students in the school.

Adrienne looked up out of her daze as if she wondered if I knew anything at all. "Holly? No. She wouldn't be up there. Some of the other senior girls, though. They're rolling on ecstasy."

I didn't ask which girls she was talking about, and hoped she wouldn't tell me. "I heard that was becoming a thing." There had been some mushrooms for a while when I'd been a student, but I hadn't known anyone who did anything like ecstasy. It had mostly just been alcohol and pot when I was coming up.

"Everyone was smoking. They had a gas mask, Keith and those guys. Like from World War II." She held up her hands to demonstrate the mask's surprising proportions. "They set it up so they could smoke with it. Everyone was taking turns wearing it in one of the bedrooms. Then Jenna put it on and started running around and sneaking up on people. And then she was just standing there in the middle of the living room and they were lighting the snorkel thing and smoke was filling the eye holes."

I imagined the smallest cheerleader standing atop a pyramid in the middle of the gym wearing an anteater-style gas mask, smoke seeping out around its edges. "Sounds unsettling."

"It was. It was—" Her gaze became unfixed and she couldn't seem to find the word she was looking for. "It seemed unreal. I only wore it for a minute. Everyone said 'Adrienne, you have to,' and 'we have to get Adrienne to do it,' so I did. They only shotgunned me once. Then I started coughing really bad and they had to take it off. And then I threw up on the carpet. Everyone was laughing. Then one of the guys who lives there was yelling at me, like 'you have to get the 'eff out of here,' and I wanted to leave but Camilla and Renee wanted to stay, and so—"

"So you came down here to the laundry room and found your English teacher waiting on his dryer."

"And then that." A few of the tears that had been brimming began to roll down her face.

In class, I would have handed her a tissue or offered her a pass to the counselors, but here neither option was available. "Renee Prescott?" I asked, instead.

She nodded and I felt myself wince. Renee Prescott wasn't the kind of girl I would have expected Adrienne Gallegos to pass her time with.

"Are you okay now?"

"Some of the senior girls do cocaine," she said, probably more for the sake of her own processing than for me to understand.

"Don't do cocaine."

She regarded me again as if I didn't understand

anything. Since I hadn't said "don't do" with respect to anything else, had I tacitly given her permission to drink, smoke weed, and pop ecstasy?

"I'm not planning to." There was indignation in her voice, as if I hadn't been paying attention as she'd been speaking; as if I'd somehow forgotten who she was.

I cocked an eyebrow as if she'd forgotten who *I* was.

"I won't do cocaine," she said.

The power going into the dryer cut out and it spun to a stop. In the room's new silence we could hear the thump of music from above. Standing, I retrieved my basket from the top of the bank of dryers, opened my own machine's door, and began gathering my sheets. "Do you have a safe ride to get home?"

Her hand touched her front pocket where the outline of her phone stood out. "I can get one."

"Don't be afraid to call your parents if you need to." I hefted my basket.

"If I need to," she agreed.

"And if you need anything, my apartment's at the far end of the hall." I pointed toward my corner of the building. "It's the last one on the left."

She backed through the doorway to make way for me as I approached. "You're not going to tell my mom?"

"Not unless you want me to," I said as I squeezed past her. Then, over my shoulder: "Be your best self."

BACK IN MY APARTMENT, I thought about Nathaniel Hawthorne. Not his novel *The Scarlet Letter*, but a short story he wrote called "Young Goodman Brown." In the tale, the young, "good man" stepped out of his house one evening despite the protests of his wife to join his outwardly virtuous neighbors in a night of sinful revel. How similar had Adrienne's experience of the evening been to the experience of the story's title character? How eerily similar was her experience to the experience I'd had in high school?

My mind went to what she'd said about Jenna Curtis. What was the best word to describe the image of the tiniest cheerleader in a powder blue and white outfit wearing a gas mask during a halftime show? Was it "grotesque" or "surreal"? Was there a better word to describe the incongruity? Beyond the image of the diminutive cheerleader, what could be done with the mental picture of Adrienne, perhaps the most promising student in her class, sitting in a classroom desk with her pencils, pens, paper and notebooks arrayed before her and a rubber gas mask obscuring her face? There had been days this semester when every other student but her in the class had missed my joke—she'd sometimes been so astute it felt as if there was a second adult in the room.

I opened the copy of the junior-level textbook I kept at home and leafed toward the story. What I couldn't wrap my head around was the duality of the lives people live. I didn't understand how Adrienne, who I could always count on to do the reading, who wrote near-flawlessly, could pass her Saturday nights with Keith Durham, who lit firecrackers in the lunch room and read at a fifth-grade level, or Renee Prescott, who, if the rumors were true, had blown three members of the boys soccer team on a bus trip back from Hutchinson after the second match of this year's season. And I didn't have trouble coming up with analogous situations from my own teenage experience. How many disparities between what I had expected and what had taken place had I known? Good people behaved in ways that were out of character all the time. Hadn't Mrs. Cates, my tenth-grade English instructor, the woman who taught me *To Kill a Mockingbird,* been caught giving a blow job to Associate Principal Fredericks my senior year? Hadn't Mr. Meyers, my eighth-grade physical science teacher, an assistant coach for the high school track team, been pulled over for drunk driving and found to have a prostitute in his car? And I certainly wasn't innocent. How many times had I, an Honors English Student of the Year, driven home across town—or into town from fifteen miles out in the county—after a night of drinking? How many times had my friends and I pulled a 'Hey you' to solicit some collarless Hispanic guy in a liquor store parking lot to go buy for us? In high school I had never taken Spanish and couldn't have asked where a bathroom was if I'd needed to go, but I'd learned how to say 'Veinticuatro cervezas, por favor' while holding out a twenty in a liquor store's parking lot. And I hadn't been a habitual user, but I'd smoked some weed of a Saturday night or two, hadn't I?

I fell to thinking of further perversities and misalignments: the fact that I, expected by so many to go so far after my senior year, was instead teaching English at the failing high school I had graduated from; the fact that in my teaching of English, I was forbidden the use of novels, plays, and works of poetry—the bedrock foundations of our literature and towering accomplishments of our language. The fact that the person forbidding my teaching of that literature was titled the *Head of Literacy*...

I closed the book after finishing the story. Hawthorne knew something about the dualities and contradictions of human nature—our moral failings and hypocrisy. It was all there, everything I knew but couldn't quite articulate, documented even if it wasn't fully explained. "Young Goodman Brown," I thought, putting the book back up on my shelf. It occurred to me I might teach it to my students. It would fit with my *Crucible* unit and discussions of the Puritans. I *would* teach it.

5

"You're out early," Trent Richardson observed when I walked into his trailer before school on Monday morning. "And in the wrong neck of the woods."

It was just after seven, and, having mulled a conversation with the head of the teacher's union throughout the weekend, I was, indeed, out early. I had parked in the all but empty teachers' parking lot a few minutes before, and now my shoes were wet from the morning dew I had unsettled on my hike across the West Field to the exiled teachers' trailer park.

"Cup of coffee?" he asked. The coffee was how I'd known he would be here. For the last 25 years, Mr. Richardson had kept three coffee machines, two burr grinders, a collection of mugs, and a varied inventory of cheap beans in his room, free to access for any current or former student who wanted them before school, after, during class, or over lunch. I had availed myself of this privilege a number of times as a student, but only once since becoming a teacher.

"No thanks," I said. "I just have a couple questions about Form-57s and how likely I am to get fired."

Pouring some water out of a gallon jug into the first of his machines—"Betty," if she was still the one I thought I recognized from my tenure as his student—Trent nodded. "Let me get my thinking juice going and I'd be happy to talk about it."

My father called Trent the "eunuch in chief," an appellation that connoted, if not total impotence, then at least a lack of qualities associated with testosterone and masculinity, so I had been surprised when I'd walked into AP US History on the first day of my junior year and discovered that Trent Richardson was a big, bearded, and clearly virile man. A five-year army vet, his deep baritone had regularly startled me with its incidental booming when I had been his student (no tired student ever accidentally fell asleep in his class), and watching him now as he went about the ritual of preparing his first cup of coffee of the day, the impression he gave me was more of an amicable and deeply intelligent bear in loafers, olive pants, and a tweed jacket doing a science experiment than of a castrated servant preparing tea for his queen.

"What do you need to know," he asked after he'd finished his ritual and settled behind his desk.

"Our head of literacy took issue with one of my lessons last week and wrote me up for teaching off-curriculum," I said.

"And you're wanting to contest it?"

I shook my head. "I'm wanting to know what it means."

"That depends. Are you a good teacher?"

"Not the worst."

Trent sipped from his mug, set it down. "Then it doesn't mean anything."

"Nothing?"

"I have six of 'em," he said. "There are people teaching in this building who have more than ten. Sherry Coroner over in Art has sixteen or seventeen, and Doyle Walters in science, before he retired, had almost two dozen." He clucked his tongue. "I just talked to him over the summer. He's still sorry he wasn't able to pick up his twenty-fourth."

"So it's not a three-strikes and you're out kind of thing?"

"Noooo," said Trent, drawing out the vowel. "More of a symbolic swat on your hind quarters. Documentation in case the district wants to build a case against someone with tenure, sure, but unless you touched someone inappropri-ately or you're entirely incompetent, they're not going to do that."

"This is my fourth year. I'm not tenured."

He shrugged. "So you'll be tenured next year."

"But I'm not planning to come back. I'm applying to law schools and maybe a couple of grad programs this winter."

Trent looked up, swinging his beard out over his collar. "So you won't be here. What's your concern?"

"I just figured, what with it being my last year and all, I'd ignore everything Hirsche and the Central Office said and I'd really teach. You know, all the stuff they don't want us to do. I wanted to make sure they wouldn't kick me to the curb before the year was over."

Trent tilted back in his chair and roared. He had the kind of laugh that filled a person's heart with joy.

"Noooo," he said again. "No. The admins can't replace the teachers they've got quitting mid-year of their own accord. They're not going to fire somebody competent and try to put a long-term sub in place. Do your teaching, Mr. Able. Put in your notice before the end of April and they won't be able to fire you." He laughed again and wiped his eye.

"Thank you," I said. I turned toward the door, and Trent, who was still laughing, called out after me.

"Seriously. You had me worried for a second. You teach 'em good over there in English, Mr. Able. Be a shame to lose you, but I know this place isn't for everyone." He saluted me. "I thank you for your service and wish you all the luck in the world."

IN CONTINUING to teach the old, traditional curriculum in the weeks that followed, I wasn't so much following a new plan as adhering to an established one, but I was doing so with a renewed—or perhaps brand new—sense of purpose. In my regular-track English II classes, I moved from my preliminary lessons on the Puritans to teaching "Young Goodman Brown" and a couple other stories by Nathaniel Hawthorne. In my honors section, we moved from The Rhetoric of the American Revolution to The Fundamentals of Argumentative Writing. During my plan periods and some of my time after school, I began tuning up my unit on American Romantic Poetry and Essays. The principals came in, and for the most part—especially with out-of-the-know principals from departments like Math and Science—I snowed them. They nodded their heads, checked their boxes, and left my room. The principals who were in-the-know—like Mr. Avery, the English department principal, and Mr. Russel—betrayed their understanding of my transgression with disapproving frowns and tilted heads, but checked their boxes and left as well. I could always sense, at some point midway through their visits, a moment when they acquiesced to the quality of my instruction. My classes were orderly, my students more participatory and involved than many in other rooms in the building, and I seldom— almost never—wrote discipline referrals. So long as I was running a tight ship and the students appeared to be learning, why would the principals unleash a swell that might rock my boat, upending my students into their offices?

When Valerie Stephens came into my room with a letter to the editor of the *Post-Dispatch* that she, Mrs. Rosenbaum, and Mrs. Dennison had composed, I signed it. Gradually, as time passed and I never received a follow-up email—and, indeed, as the frequency of the administrative walkthroughs seemed to lessen—I began to get the sense that I had won— that I might be allowed to serve out my year left alone to teach in whatever fashion I liked. Then, on the last Friday of October, the Head of Literacy walked into my classroom.

It was, again, my athlete-heavy section of English II. Having finished our short stories and completed a little bit of pre-writing, we had begun reading Arthur Miller's *The Crucible*. We were midway through the first act, approaching the revealing scene between John Proctor and Abigail Williams when their affair becomes evident. Perhaps owing to the fact it was Friday, or because of the game scheduled for that night, or because things had gone so well with my honors students that I had failed to set the hook properly with my regulars—or for any one of the other myriad reasons a play can go well in one class and poorly in another —things weren't going very well. Javi, assigned the part of Thomas Putnam, accidentally read over his friend Chris, assigned Parris, for the second time and threw up his hands in frustration. "Why are we even doing this?" he cried. "There's too many 'P' names. It's *confusing*."

Instinctively, my eyes went to Mrs. Hirsche and her clipboard at the back of the room. She was making a note. The thing to do was slow down and answer his question, maybe take a few minutes to list the relevant 'P'-named characters on the board and describe them so that my students might better differentiate them when their eyes fell on their names on the page. But I didn't want to slow down. I didn't want to admit things weren't going smoothly while the Head of Literacy was in my room.

"Stick with me," I said instead of taking the proper time. "It becomes more clear. Trust me."

To which Javi, who hadn't been given much reason to trust many people in his life, responded by flipping his pencil, striking Tristan Malone on the side of his head. Tristan, bigger, heavier, and less inclined to air grievances verbally than Javi, responded to this provocation by rising partway out of his chair to swipe Javi upside his head— payback and more, as everyone in the room knew Javi had a tube of expensive product in his backpack he brought to school for the express purpose of sculpting his hair into its meticulous arrangement after zero-hour weights.

"The hell?" he said, turning and raising his arm. And then I was wading forward between the desks and back-packs and loose books and dropped pencils, saying "Whoa" and "Hey" as I came between them, spending the last few minutes of Mrs. Hirsche's observation talking them down and divvying out new parts in the play since both boys now refused to read.

"I ENJOYED your letter to the editor," said the Head of Literacy an hour and a half later.

"Thank you." In truth, beyond this present comment,

there'd been no response to the letter that I knew of. None from the editors, no follow-up letters from readers, no response from the Central Office or admins in our building. A school board meeting had come and gone without the letter being mentioned.

We were in the principals' conference room, the closed door giving our meeting an air of disciplinary action—though, again, there were no principals in the room. "You clearly care about your teaching. Do you mind if I ask you a question?"

"Shoot."

"What's more important to you, the material or the students?"

The question smelled suspicious; it held within its confines, I suspected, some sort of trap. "The students," I said carefully. "That's why you teach them the most high-quality material you can find. To enrich their lives."

She pursed her lips and nodded—this was the type of answer she had come to expect from me. As I watched, she sketched a little tic-tac-toe board on a sheet of paper between us, then, as if pre-ordaining whatever match might have been played between us a cat game, arced a swirl through it. She looked up.

"Are you teaching for *them*, or are you teaching for *you*?"

"Them, obviously."

An infinitesimal hint of a smile appeared on her lips, then vanished. She seemed to become a little harder, a little more severe. "The levels of frustration and disengagement I saw today would seem to indicate your material wasn't reaching them."

I tried to explain that the play typically began slowly, but that in the past my students had caught on and become more interested as the second and third acts passed, but she was dismissive of this line of reasoning. She cut me off before I had time to finish delivering it.

"How many students do you have in that room who read three or more levels below grade level?"

"About a third," I hazarded.

"Thirteen," she said. "Almost half. And do you know how many read six or more levels below grade level?"

"Four?"

"Six. Do you think those six students—" she handed a copy of my roster, with six names highlighted, across the table so I could see it—"who read at third and fourth grade levels, do you think *they* are enjoying the experience of reading The Crucible? Do you think it will *hook* them? Or do you agree with me that likely the experience is most entirely lost on them?"

"We're reading most of the play aloud—"

"So they don't have to read it themselves, but can use their peers' voices as a crutch."

"—and I think there's a lot to be said for the age-appropriateness of the material, and how it dove-tails with the junior US History curriculum. It's cross-curricular."

Material being 'cross-curricular' was formerly an argument that had held weight in the building, but it didn't seem to now. "How many weeks are you spending on this? In the event a student doesn't get on board with this unit—or can't get on board—then how many weeks of instruction will you have lost? Five? Six?"

"Four," I said. "Two to read the play, one to break it down for discussion and review, and one to write a paper."

I thought she might comment here on the inappropriateness of my assigning a written paper in defiance of the administration's injunctions against them, but she seemed content to let this violation go. She smiled.

"Four weeks," she said. "This reminds me of an ongoing conversation I've been having with a couple of your fellow teachers. About how much of our instructional time we squander when we teach longer units like novels by Harper Lee and plays by Shakespeare."

My face, I'm sure, betrayed my reaction to this assertion. Of all of the contradictions and ironies presented by our ironically titled Head of Literacy, this must have been the greatest. "So you're a 'no' with regard to Shakespeare?"

She seemed to relish the opportunity to respond. "Oh, I'm not the only one who thinks we should stop teaching the bard."

She reached into her bag, pulled out a glossy-covered book, and passed it across the table to me. Its title, in a bold, all-capped, sans-serif font, read *Stories Don't Matter in the Real World.* "It's by a teacher in California. William Gramley. He teaches in a district with demographics similar to ours." I took it, turned it over to see a list of blurbs on its back, and then flipped it open to the spot held by a popular online bookstore's bookmark: the table of contents. There were nine chapters listed, the first of which shared its title with the book. Scanning down, I also read "Education: Myths vs. Realities," "Classical Education vs. The Modern Classroom," "Learning for the Real World," "Nonfiction in the ELA Classroom," "Vocabulary Conundrums," "English in the Age of the Internet," "Passing the Test," and, in the last position, "Does Shakespeare Still Matter in the Real World?"

I heard the ambient buzzing in the conference room grow louder. Mrs. Hirsche was still talking, but I couldn't hear what she was saying. I felt the surface of my skin go hot, then cold, and after a moment had to remind myself to breath. Mrs. Hirsche continued to speak. "—no clear relationships between reading these long works by the likes of

Shakespeare and Arthur Miller and any sort of real-world preparedness. There's no research-based connection between reading long works and doing anything that looks even slightly marketable or remunerative in the modern job market."

"Does everything have to be remunerative?" I asked, sounding more feeble and far-away than I wanted to sound. "Does everything have to be about making money?"

Mrs. Hirsche tilted her head, modulating her voice in a way that was almost sympathetic. "But don't you see that's a question you can afford to ask? We both know what your father does for a living, and more than half of your students are second and third generation immigrants. A significant number don't have parents who speak English at home."

The cold feeling on the surface of my skin began sinking inward. I began to feel numb. Mrs. Hirsche's voice, partially because she had pitched it more softly, but also because everything in the room now seemed muffled, sounded far away. The bell rang. I had a class to teach. I rose, tried to hand the book back to her, but she shook her head and pressed it back into my hands. "Keep it," she said. "I ordered it for you."

I TAUGHT MY LAST CLASS—OR went through the motions of teaching it—and sat in the chair behind my desk for a long time after the cries of the students had faded after the building let out.

Are you teaching for them, or are you teaching for you, the Head of Literacy had asked, and whether wittingly or un-, she had struck on the ideal key to disarm me, cut as it was to resonate with my inborn cynicism and knock me off of a high horse I hadn't known I was sitting on. Because as much as I professed to hating the job—and as much as I had insisted it was temporary and that I would be leaving for either grad school or law school in the fall, I *had* begun to take pride in my work. To feel righteous about it, even. She had my number when she accused me of teaching for myself more than my students: that was a jab that connected. And then to get out that glossy-covered book and unbalance the other side of my previously balanced equation—to argue that what I was doing *didn't matter*—that *Stories Didn't Matter*? An absolute haymaker. A consciousness-obliterating knockout punch. Even now, when I stood up in my classroom and tried to shake it off, I felt dizzy.

Passing the window at Wonder's Bakery after I'd driven home and parked my car in the Douglas Building's back lot, I saw Lauren West sitting at a table reading a book. She had a cup of tea with one of the establishment's famous spiced biscotti angled across its saucer. Under normal circumstances I might have continued walking, or, at most, tapped on the glass to wave. But I still heard that muffled buzzing that I'd been hearing since my meeting with the Head of Literacy, and the air around my head felt thick and cottony, a sensation not unlike being a little bit drunk. Situated as she was, holding and devoting all of her attention to her book, she appeared antithetical to everything the Head of Literacy had earlier argued. Following the logic of a dream—indeed, I felt like I was dreaming—I turned to find the bakery's door and a few moments later stood in front of her.

"Good book?" I asked.

Her eyes finished crossing the line she was on and moved across another. She put a finger between the book's pages and closed its covers. "Yes," she said vaguely, and when she looked up it was with annoyance. Continuing to follow my dream-logic, I decided to disregard this senti-ment. "I had the strangest meeting earlier today. Do you mind—"

Even as I sat, I understood how I was importuning her, but the muffled buzzing was muting my normal inclination toward social reserve, and my need to unload was too great. Plus, a shadowy half-thought: hadn't she importuned me at the Oasis, when I had been grieving, and hadn't I taken time to give her some of the low-down on the school? A measure of reciprocity seemed due.

She lowered her book. "What's up?"

Briefly, I outlined for her the meeting, from its opening exchange of lukewarm pleasantries to the Head of Literacy's concerns about my lowest-achieving students to her handing me a copy of *Stories Don't Matter in the Real World*. Mentioning the title of the book, I remembered that I had it with me. Dead-handed, I lifted it out of my bag and hoisted it for her to see.

Rather than betraying any of the sympathetic responses I had expected—incredulity, horror, outrage, or some mix of all three—Lauren remained impassive while I spoke. It seemed there was a dream-logic to this as well. Had she become an octopus or a hydra, or if we had picked up rackets and walked across the floor to play badminton over the pastry case, I wouldn't have been surprised at all. But instead of any of these more plausible alternatives, she began to nod her head in agreement. "I can see some of her points," she said, and by the way the atmosphere in the room became even more wooly and thick, I sensed the possibility I was having a dream ebb away—felt a rising awareness I was involved in a nightmare.

"We do teach too much fiction in Language Arts classes," she said. "But we've known that for a while."

I stared at her dumbly.

"If not too much fiction, then definitely not enough non-fiction," she amended, less for my benefit than because she seemed to be clarifying her own thoughts.

"You think we should do more of the short passage stuff? All test-prep, all the time?"

She shook her head hard enough to rattle the tea cup she still held aloft on its saucer. "God no. We should be doing longer works. But more of them should be nonfiction. Biographies and histories. Long-form journalism. Pro-and-con analysis of sophisticated topics. I mean, fiction does it for a lot people, but it doesn't do it for everyone. Plus, too much of it's by DWMs."

The acronym gave me a moment's pause. WMDs had been much in the news a few years before, and this similar-sounding abbreviation threw me. "DW—" I started to ask, but finished deciphering the code before I hit the third letter.

"Dead White Men," she said, her tone blasé. "Too much of the fiction we teach in schools perpetuates harmful cultural myths. The patriarchy, white supremacy—" she hadn't been looking at me—she was lecturing as if by rote—but glanced toward my face now and caught my expression. "You don't think so? Maybe you haven't noticed. Or maybe you just don't mind, since you *are* a white man. Plus, you're a content teacher."

"We're all content teachers."

"I mean in the dichotomy between 'student' and 'content.' There are people in the profession for the students, and others in it for the material. You're clearly the latter."

I heard an echo, here, of one of the Head of Literacy's arguments against me from earlier, and Lauren's use of *clearly* dully registered as the kind of word I would have circled in a student paper—an assertion of absolute certainty the arguer didn't have the absolute evidence to back up—but my field of vision was narrowing and my hands, feet, arms and legs were beginning to feel remote from the rest of my body. "We teach *To Kill a Mockingbird,*" I said impotently.

"Name two other women we teach novels or plays by on a regular basis."

"Lorraine..."

"Hansberry? Can you name the play?"

It was a second semester work. The title was from a Hughes poem, but I couldn't bring it to mind. "Women haven't been in a position to write as many long works as men," I said, trying to mount, if not an argument, then at least an explanation.

Lauren's eyes flashed. "Bullshit," she said primly. "There are plenty of long works by women. We don't teach them because we don't want to. This school district, just like districts across the country, doesn't want to spend the money to purchase books by women. Because we don't value them. Because of DWMs, the patriarchy, and white supremacy. In a way, I applaud the Head of Literacy. It might be that we need to take a wrecking ball to the whole system."

DWMs. The patriarchy and white supremacy. Book banning justified. *QED.* "You don't think we should teach Shakespeare? Or The Crucible?"

She set down her saucer and reached back with both of her hands to check the clasp holding back her hair. The conversation seemed to have become heated to me—my hands were clammy and I could feel perspiration beginning to soak my t-shirt under my button-up—but Lauren was wearing a sleeveless shirt and her arms, the declivities of her armpits, and her shoulders appeared papery dry. "Romeo and Juliet. A lot of phallic swordplay; conflations of misogyny, violence, and sex; the wise nurse—maybe the wisest character in the play—gets put down by everybody, and in most productions they play her as a fool. Rosalind isn't interested in Romeo and gets treated as a cold fish because of it. Capulet barters his daughter off without giving her any say in the matter, and the girl throws her life away at the end because she thinks the boy is dead. Seems like it has male fantasy written all over it, doesn't it? And The Crucible? Too easy. The girls are all liars, the female character with the most autonomy gets called a whore, and the pedophilic white guy who, if you really look at it, started the whole thing, gets to redeem himself and die as a hero."

If these struck me as a somewhat selective reads of the texts, I recognized they were valid and supportable nonetheless. And I didn't have the wherewithal in front of Lauren West and her cool, dismantling arguments to disagree with her. In addition to the cold sweat draining from my armpits, I could now feel the blood draining from my face. My field of vision was narrowing further, Lauren becoming a Bugs Bunny centered in a constricting field of black. I might be in danger, I thought, of passing out. I stood up. "That's true," I said. "That's all true." I lurched toward the bakery's inside door leading to the vestibule and mid-building elevator, pressed the button with the heel of my hand and, when the doors opened, stumbled in to lean my arm and forehead against one of the lift's three mirrored walls. Then I was letting myself out and sleepwalking down the hall into my apartment, finding my way to my couch, and then falling twice-over: first onto it, and then into a sweaty, restless, dreamless sleep.

6

I awoke in the dark, the shadows of my under-watered plants moving across my wall in yellow light as cars passed on the street below. Above, I could hear the pounding music and running feet of a late-stage college party. The right side of my jaw ached, and I felt, when I tried to sit up, the tightness of a crick along my spine stretching between the middle of my back and the base of my skull. The time on my DVD player read 11:43.

The lights on, bathroom visited, I found three messages on my phone, each from Garret, asking if I wanted to go out to the Oasis. I ignored them, and powered it off. I drank down a glass of water, ate an overripe banana, and, after unsuccessfully scanning the shelves of my fridge and freezer for something more sustaining, settled on a bowl of Cheerios for dinner. The new book I had been reading since finishing *Lord Jim* was sitting on my end table, but a glance told me I wouldn't find any pleasure in picking it up right now. Looking toward my bookshelves reminded me of the William Gramley book tucked into my bag and filled me with fear. I picked up the remote from its place beside the

TV, instead, and flipped until I found a channel showing late-night reruns of last-century sit-coms: *Cheers*, *Mad about You*, *Friends*, *Frasier*. I watched these, eating another bowl of cereal and a bowl of badly frost-burned ice cream while I did so, listening as the sounds of the building gradually swelled, then receded, until sometime after four o'clock in the morning when I finally went to bed.

I didn't wake until almost one o'clock the next afternoon, the first time I had slept past noon since I was in college, I was sure. I swigged the bottom inch of a container of orange juice from my fridge to finish the bottle, ate another bowl of Cheerios, dressed myself in jeans and a sweatshirt, and walked outside to find that the fall had begun in earnest overnight, every third or fourth tree streaked with orange or red in the same way my father's once dark hair had begun to streak silver in the last few years. As I watched, leaves from the trees planted along the street fell steadily, arcing to the ground. I walked for perhaps half an hour, and when I returned home, lifted a binder-clipped stack of student papers—'honors' section essays over *The Crucible*—from my desk and shuffled through them, hearing in this shuffle some of the buzzing I had heard the day before. I found in my quick perusal what I had secretly known I would: that, while a few were good, and a couple even admirable, the bulk were poorly done. Many were unpardonably short, and a number made it clear that their young authors clearly hadn't understood the play. Some hadn't even understood the assignment. I set them down, picked up the remote control, and watched television for another couple hours.

I went downstairs and across the street to get take-out from Dos Amigos as the daylight fell away, sitting at the bar and watching rerun futbol on Telemundo while I waited for my food to arrive. I carried it in its white plastic sack back across the street and up my flights of stairs, eating in front of reruns of *Friends* and *Seinfeld,* passing the second half of my weekend in a similar manner to the way I had passed the first between walks, television, bowls of Cheerios, and sleep. When I woke Monday morning, I wasn't tired or angry or frustrated or hungry, but hollowed-out, suffused with that 1st- or 2nd-year teacher's terror that I might stand in front of my first class and find that I had nothing to say.

I ate the last of my Cheerios dry—my milk had run out the previous evening, and I hadn't wanted to run to the store —and drove to school steadily, watching the lights turn yellow and then red in front of me, noted the way more leaves in the park had turned yellow and red beside me. When I arrived in class I found, as I always had, that my words would come—did come—that I could rely on a sort of deep-set auto-pilot. That I could teach like a high-func-tioning alcoholic, or, I suppose more accurately, depressive.

The daily actions of teaching—greeting my students, smiling at their quips and questions, delivering my lessons, pausing to refocus them when they fell off of task and calm them when they became too high-spirited—were exhausting to me, though. By the middle of my second block I had a headache; before the end of my third I was having trouble disguising my irritability. I was short with my fourth block students, yelled at my fifth. At the end of the day I didn't lie down on my couch at home so much as collapse onto it. When I woke it was after seven, almost dark outside, the shadows of my dying houseplants creeping across my wall and ceiling as evening coffee drinkers arrived and departed from Wonder's below and diners pulled up in front of Dos's across the street. I decided to go to the popular Mexican place myself; ordered a smothered burrito, a bag of chips, and a Styrofoam cup of salsa. I passed five more hours watching television on my couch and went to bed sometime after one.

The following days passed in much the same manner, with my headaches receding somewhat, the naps I took after school getting longer, and the hour at which I went to bed for the night creeping beyond two. The pain I had first noticed in my jaw after my first long nap increased. The feeling of having given my all wasn't foreign to me: I had been an athlete growing up, and had been similarly drained by two-a-day basketball practices, overtime Friday night games, and all-day track meets in the heat of May. The difference was that in those cases the exhaustion had always been balanced by a countervening inflow of strength. Hard work's reward: the satisfaction of a job well done. Now when I opened an eye before eight in the evening, it drifted down to the last book leaning against the others on the bottom of my living room bookshelf, William Gramley's *Stories Don't Matter in the Real World*, and what dregs of strength I had reaped from napping seemed to go out of me and I surrendered myself to another half hour's bout of sleep.

This was my pattern for the next few weeks. Teaching for eight hours, sleeping for four or five, waking to spend several hours living my 'other' life in my apartment until falling asleep again sometime between two and four to get a few hours rest before school, so that my days became bifurcated and surreal, school miserable, my evenings alone, my eerie dreams set in abandoned, subterranean, and subaquatic locations.

Finally, the ache in my jaw became so painful I had to do something about it. I made an appointment with Dr. Hill, my longtime dentist.

"October into November. The teacher's vortex of doom," he joked as he finished his metal-hooked inspection.

I rinsed my mouth and spit cherry-colored saliva into his little porcelain fountain. "How's that?"

"My wife used to be a teacher," he explained. "Twenty-six years. 2nd and 3rd grade. Everyone starts with great expectations in August, and by the end of October the kids have worn them down to a nub so it's all they can do to hope for Christmas break. You're grinding your molars in your sleep. I'm going to set you up with an appliance. I give a lot of them to teachers this time of year."

He rolled away in his chair to open a drawer on the other side of the room. I touched the outside of my jaw exploratorily, visualized the tiny galaxy of pain swirling out from beneath my back teeth.

"You play football?"

"In middle school." When I looked up he tossed me a baggie with something yellow in it.

"That's an old-fashioned mouthguard. You can dip it in some boiling water and fit it yourself. It'll hold you until the appliance we order comes in."

I recognized it, of course. Remembered boiling one in the 7th grade and squeezing it between my teeth before cutting off its long dipping stem and allowing it to cool.

I stood, and found I was as unsteady on my feet as I felt in my mind. It was after four and I was due for my afternoon meeting with my couch. "How long will it be?"

"Two or three weeks. Any longer than that and you call me." He offered his hand. "See you this weekend?"

The look I gave him must have told him I didn't know what he was talking about.

"Jim Morris's thing. Birthday-slash-retirement? Anne

sent out the invitations... must have been six weeks back. I thought surely you'd—"

"I'm a little behind on checking my mail."

He grinned, shook his head. "Vortex of doom," he said, and he guided me out. "Don't let the kids get you down. Holidays are coming!"

There was, as I had expected there would be, an embossed envelope with the Morris's country club address stamped on it situated low in the stack of my mail when I returned home. While I had continued dutifully to unlock my box and collect my mail every day in the last several weeks—I had red-enveloped DVDs coming once or twice a week, two credit card bills, student loan statements, and a few utilities to watch out for—the bulk of my mail I had allowed to accumulate. By the size of the stack, I estimated I hadn't opened anything beyond the essential since the week Bryce had rolled his truck over. The Morris's invitation I had likely taken for a high-end credit card offer.

It was, as Dr. Hill had suggested, a birthday and retirement party. I didn't want to go, but to skip the occasion would be a social misstep, insulting to the Morrises and shameful for my father.

I tried to call Eloise, Jim's secretary, so as to RSVP more discretely than calling Anne Morris's home number listed on the invitation, but Eloise *nuh-uh*ed me, telling me the dinner was in Anne's province, she wasn't involved. "I'm just his *work* wife, honey. Lucky I got an invitation myself." I called the number on the invite, tried to offer my profound and heartfelt apology, and was told my father had already RSVP'd on my behalf. I would have a place beside him and Sharon at the head table.

"Thank you, Mrs. Morris," I said, and "I'm sorry aga-"

"That's quite alright, dearie," she told me. "As long as

you don't have a date you want to show up with, everything should work out just fine."

A date, I thought, clicking off my phone. *In this town?*

I looked up and saw that it was half-past five. I set my phone to silent, lifted my blanket from its place on my couch's arm, and laid down for my first bout of sleep of the night.

7

My father hadn't always lived at the country club. He moved to his condo overlooking the fourth hole of the course the year after my parents' divorce, when I was a sophomore in college, so the amount of time I had 'lived' at the club was limited to a couple of summers and two or three Christmas breaks during my undergrad. My grandfather had lived at the club for the entirety of my remembered life before he passed, though, and my parents were members, of course. So my memories of going to the club for birthday parties, Sunday brunches, Christmas mornings, Easter egg hunts, and the like were many. On the evening of Jim Morris's Birthday-slash-retirement party, driving south out of town, over the bridge, east onto River Road, and through the gate with its little white guard house flanked by split-rail fences felt eerily like returning home.

The sun was setting as I parked in the clubhouse lot, and a pair of carts were driving off toward the near row of the club's original premium condominiums, the ones with views of the first three holes of the course, the second of which my grandfather had occupied for thirty-four years. The other cars in the lot where I parked were chiefly luxury models, Cadillacs, Lexuses, and Mercedes, with a black Jaguar and a classic Corvette mixed in for good measure. The couples getting out of them wore suits and tuxedos, long dresses and high heels, shining watches, and dangling bracelets and necklaces. I was still exhausted, living my bifurcated, two-phase lifestyle, and was dimly glad I had elected to wear the nicer of my two sport coats and the least-scuffed of my dress shoes. As sometimes happens when you're very tired, every-thing, the details of hood ornaments, the edges of buildings, the quality of the evening's light, seemed especially sharp, and before the façade of the clubhouse I could see that destiny was a force made up of two component parts—time and money—and that it was inexorable. Someday it would wear me down. Someday soon, perhaps. I wondered if—worried that—everyone inside would be able to see me as clearly as I could see the details of my surroundings and discern my destiny. I worried they would see how tired and hollow I was: a poor teacher, not someone who belonged *here*.

I said good evening to Raul, the concierge, at the entrance desk and made my way up the broad and familiar flight of stairs. Walking into the Buffalo Bill Room at the age of twenty-six filled me with a sensation of Déjà vu, the room still decorated the same way it had been twenty and ten years before when I was six and then sixteen. I found myself unconsciously standing up straighter, pulling my lips back to smile, looking out for hands to shake. In this arena I was no longer myself, but a coached representative of my mother and father's. An appendage. Had I been more possessed of my self, I might have resented this state of affairs; my state of mind being what it was, I welcomed it.

My father's son was a role I could play, after all, and I was otherwise uncertain of who I was at the moment. So I shook hands with Mr. Bauer and Mr. Shelton, nodded and exchanged *hellos* and *yeses* and *I remembers* with their wives. I lifted my hand in acknowledgement of the Powells and the Ottermeyers. From Vicky, the waitress who had once served me orange juices and milk, I ordered a bourbon and Coke, one of the three or four staple drinks men at the club ordered on occasions like this, and I briefly, unobtrusively slipped myself into a break in a conversation Mrs. Morris was having to thank her for her invitation. Jim Jr was at the bar; my pointed finger acknowledged him and promised my intention to talk to him later in the evening.

I shook hands with my father, let him pull me in tight for a one-armed embrace, and stood by as an extra listener in the conversation he, Jim Morris, and a few of the other men were having. Vicky arrived with her tray and handed me my drink, from which I took my first tentative, reas-suring sips. The conversation the men were having was the inverse of one I had heard in Wonder's Bakery, read in the *Post-Dispatch*, and listened to on the radio news in the last year. The subject matter was the ongoing consequence of the financial collapse, but here the market-quake wasn't a tragedy but a rare and golden opportunity: a chance these men had had to reap windfalls. They named stocks and funds, compared prices, and described deep discounts. Abe Sterling said he'd gotten "six or seven steals." John Peters had made enough to finish off his kids' college funds and finance his next two summers' vacations. My father, perhaps due to my presence at his elbow, kept mum, but Jim Morris Sr. expounded gleefully about how he'd improved several positions. "I wouldn't be retiring this year if I hadn't," he said. The men raised their glasses and toasted the crash.

A glass was tapped, we found our seats, and, the hors d'oeuvres portion of the evening over, the first courses of the meal and opening speeches began in earnest. I dispatched my gazpacho, ate my roasted chicken and vegetable medley, sat through the first and second round of tributes, and slipped downstairs before the second entrée.

I was only going to take a break for a few minutes—hit the downstairs head and perhaps linger at the window overlooking the swimming pool—but the glass-paneled door to the club's little library-reading room was open and the light was on, so I decided to step in.

What was it I had so righteously asked of the Head of Literacy? *Does everything have to be about making money?* It did, of course. Part of my own love of reading had been kindled by this very room with its mahogany table, leather chairs, and leather-bound books. The Rolex-wearing men who had perused their newspapers in this room with their black-socked ankles balanced on their gray-slacked knees. *Writing short stories for popular magazines kept F Scott Fitzgerald in champagne and hotel rooms in Paris,* Mrs. Unger had told my eleventh-grade honors section. For me, books had always been tied to wealth. I had even nurtured literary ambitions of my own. Less ambitious ambitions than F Scott, to be sure: I had imagined, pragmatically, that I might earn my living early and retire before setting out on my literary career. That if I lived modestly, I might put in my own time as a lawyer for twenty or twenty-five years, then begin to scratch away at my own book. I told my father that English majors scored higher on the LSAT than history, philosophy, or poli-sci degree-holders, but it had been my closely-held, long-term ambition that had truly inspired my choice of major. It had been in my last year of college that I had panicked and bucked the plan. Gripped by an idealistic fervor—that if I didn't live pursuing my loftiest and farthest-flung goals, I wouldn't be living at all—I had decided to apply to English grad programs and hew closer to my truest desires. Foolish, of course. The Head of Literacy had been right when she had pointed out my privileged position. Only someone so spoiled as me could have cast away so solid a plan so extravagantly. I had thrown together my grad school applications in a frenzy and asked for recommendations at the last minute, paying extra to rush copies of my less-than-stellar transcripts off to a dozen programs, and I had collected a dozen thin rejection envelopes for my efforts. Then it had been the embarrassing explanation of 'wanting a year or two off' to my father and his calling me a few days later to tell me I could probably get a job teaching in the district for a year or two if I wanted. Plains City was hard-up for teachers and qualified as at-risk; degree-holding college graduates without teaching credentials could sign contracts and be paid as full-time teachers provided they took a few online courses along the way. My father had paused and cleared his throat before he told me the pay would be less than thirty thousand dollars a year, but at twenty-two, recently shut-out by a dozen grad programs, with credit card bills coming in and student loan payments about to start, twenty-eight thousand dollars a year had sounded like a lot of money to me.

The men I had seen reading in this room had never taken down and read the *books*, I realized as I looked around now. The leather-bound volumes here weren't vessels for storing or conveying knowledge, but signifiers of wealth. Not much beyond the *Wall Street Journal*, the *Financial Times*, or the occasional copy of *The Economist* was ever read in here. Maybe my own reading of the funny pages at the back of the *Post-Dispatch*. 'Funny pages,' as in 'ha-ha.' The extent of my error began to dawn on me. The amount of time I had expended apprenticing myself to foolish dreams. The raw sum of time I had wasted. The quantity of debt I had accrued when I might have been, if not *amassing wealth*, then at least wool-gathering *something* so I might have *something* to my name.

Such were my thoughts when I heard a rapping. Staring at me almost ghoulishly through one of the panes in the glass door was Jim Jr. He stepped around the door and into the room.

"You ever mess around in here?" he asked.

Perhaps because I had been thinking of my youth, I was transported back to easter egg hunts and games of hide and seek. Times I had crawled beneath the mahogany table hiding or looking for things.

"I fingered Gina Wilbur when we were sixteen," he said. "And fucked Nicole Curtis after Prom. Right about where you're standing."

I shook my head, said *no,* shook my head again.

"Mmm," he said, pressing his fingers to his lips in a 'chef's kiss' gesture that lingered on his lips a beat too long, adding an extra, unnecessary dimension of suggestion to the gesture. "Missing out."

When I didn't say anything in response, he leaned further into the room and squinted. "You feeling alright? You look kinda spooked. Like you ate a bag of 'shrooms." He waggled his eyebrows. "You on something?" He looked back over his shoulder. "If you're holding, you can break out with me."

"I haven't been feeling well," I said. I moved my hand to my stomach for emphasis. "In fact—" I made my way to the door and he let me by. "If I don't make it back upstairs, give my dad and your parents my regards."

Jim Jr laughed as I squeezed past him, and he called after me as I made my way toward the men's room. "Will do, broseph. Will do."

I FAST-WALKED out of the club, waving away Raul's question as to whether or not everything was alright, and found myself spot-lit by one of the display lights concealed in a tuft of pampas grass outside the building. Turning to avert my eyes from its glare, I caught sight of my shadow climbing up onto the building, stretched thin and inconsequential. On its other side, the revels of the party-goers continued. It occurred to me that the Head of Literacy and William Gramley were right: no one at Jim Morris, Sr's party had needed novels, plays, or poetry to reach their advantaged positions in life. None of the doctors or lawyers or retirees living in the two- and three-story condos lining the fairways at the club needed novels. None of the local business owners or administrators from the community college or executives from the power plant or managers from the meat packing plant or agribusiness industrialists needed plays. None of the young, monied families in their blue and yellow and taupe houses on the few country club streets radiating like spokes from the course needed poetry. I drove out past the floodlit club entrance with its limestone posts anchoring the split rail fence, the aesthetically rusted tin windmill presiding, and then down the darkness of River Road, saw the false-dawn glow of the city, the smaller glow of a high school bonfire. Could a short story or play read in class improve the situation of any of the students standing around that fire? It seemed unlikely. I slowed for the curve —slowed nearly to a stop—and looked out at the fatal embankment I had so assiduously avoided glancing at on my drive out to the club. There was nothing literature could do—had done?—for Bryce Davis.

Back at my building there were open spaces in the lot. The community college kids must have been partying somewhere else. Dull and mechanical, I climbed the back stairs, pressed my key into my door's lock, and sealed myself into my book-lined fourth-floor mausoleum. The architects who had designed the Douglas Building hadn't needed literature to erect this five-story outpost on the plains. The men and women who had renovated it, first into an office building, then a varied lot of incongruous and unmatching apartments, hadn't needed to read fiction. The paved parking lot I had left my car in below, the brick roads I had driven to get home, the car itself, the plumbing that brought my water and took away my waste, the channels of electricity that allowed me to illuminate my living room, bathroom, and kitchen—that ran the refrigerator and freezer to keep my food cold and safe, my microwave and electric oven to heat it when I was hungry—the people who had developed my cellular phone, erected towers and launched satellites into space to facilitate its use even in this tiny corner of Western Kansas... none of them had needed novels, plays, or poetry.

I ate some bread with peanut butter on it, stripped off my clothes, and showered. I pulled on a pair of boxers and a t-shirt, checked my phone, and turned off my lights. A minute after I climbed into bed, my phone's light lit up my room. It buzzed.

"Can you say 'Bret and me'?" the voice on its other end asked.

"Who is this?"

"It's *Davis*. Seriously now, concentrate. We've got drinks riding and I need to know: can you say 'Bret and me'?"

I sat up in the darkness of my bedroom. "Are you on a game show?"

"I'm at a *bar* you fucking tool. Bret and me"—there was a peel of laughter in the background—"we're talking to these two chicks—*Ow! Girls! ... Ladies!* English teachers, like you, but good-looking. And we've got this bet going, so I need to know. You can't, right?"

"Can't say 'Bret and me'?"

"Yeah."

I thought a moment. "It depends."

"*Depends?* The fuck is that? Depends on *what*?"

"It depends on whether you're the subject or the object. How's this bet work?"

"If they win, we buy the next round of drinks, and if we win, they do." He lowered his voice. "I've got a side bet going. If we win, I get the tall one's number."

I nodded my head in the dark. "I understand. I know what you need to say."

"Yeah?"

"Say, '*Give me a minute, I need to go to the bar and buy you ladies a pair of drinks from Bret and me.*'"

Davis swore and the connection was severed. I looked down at my phone, folded it shut. I returned it to its place on my nightstand. This was what it had come to. This was who I was: a school-marm grammarian, repository for the arbitrary and archaic rules of the English language. Someone who could proofread a document or settle a fine point in a late-night bet, perhaps, but readily replaceable by a computer's red-underlined spell check. Not just a fool, but someone almost entirely irrelevant.

8

I woke up that night, and the next, with my heart racing, but didn't realize I had entered a new, subbasement-level lowness until I walked into the high school on Monday morning. Neither the sight of my students nor the crescendoing chorus of 'Mornings, 'Morning Mr. Ables, and Hey Ables would lift me out of my torpor. The fabric seemed torn. It wasn't only that stories didn't matter, but that nothing did. I wasn't only wasting my own time, but my students'. My father's oft-repeated claim that the public schools were little more than holding pens for the children of real working people leapt forward in my mind: I was a babysitter.

By the time I made it to my classroom, I had begun to understand how much worse my situation had become. That it was fucked—that *I* was fucked—perhaps irredeemably so. When my first-block section of jock English began coming in, I knew that whatever insulating membrane I had formerly worn that had allowed me to move through the world and interact with its people had slipped loose of my skin and was gone. I wouldn't get through the day without being cut, bruised, torn, abraded. My students, on the other hand, seemed well-sleeved. They touched one another and smiled, laughed. Spoke loudly. Dropped their bags heavily beside their desks' legs and scraped their chairs' feet against the floor. Javi, who had by turns lifted me up and driven me to frustration since the middle of August, bounded in as if he wasn't just well-sleeved, but more free from the constraints of gravity than most other people. "What's good Mr. A?" he wanted to know when he landed beside my desk.

"Good morning, Javi," I returned, and he started in on the topic of discussion we had left off on at the end of the previous week.

"So you gonna be at the game on Friday night, or what?"

The game was the annual rivalry match between Plains City and Dodge. The school, over the previous weekend, had been filled with banners and signs exhorting our football players to "Beat the Demons" and "Crush DCHS!"

I had copies I knew I had made the previous week but couldn't find, objectives on my board to update. My class would start in less than two minutes. "I'm not sure yet," I said. Then, when he opened his mouth and looked to say something more: "Actually, I'm pretty sure I can't make it." I stood and stepped away from my desk. Another day, a previous day, I might have put off his invitation with something disarming or funny. Alluded to fictitious romantic plans or expressed a desire to avoid seeing my football players suffer an embarrassing defeat—Dodge City was, at the time, undefeated, with six wins, while our Chargers, after six outings, were balanced tenuously at five hundred. I found the copies I had made on the back counter, found that I didn't want to use them. Saw that there was a stack of Mrs. Hirsche's district-approved test prep materials beside them. I picked these up as the bell rang and turned around. The rest of my students were at their desks, but Javi was still standing where I had left him. The close scrutiny of his gaze, I thought, might have impressed his science teacher.

I MEANT, by the stiff and laconic manner I adopted over the next several days, to convey to my students my state of lowness—that I was worn down, didn't have *it,* whatever *it* was. That they should be quieter and more obedient. I didn't say outright that they *owed* me—that they ought to behave better since I had been so patient and forbearing with them up to this point in the year—but that's how I felt. But this isn't how a classroom works, of course. The students aren't there to forbear, only to be borne. Perhaps sensing my desire to invert this arrangement, they acted out.

Premier among my problems was the fact of the upcoming weekend's rivalry game against Dodge City. I had come to realize, in my brief tenure as a teacher, that some school events—homecoming week, the fall musical, the Dodge City game, and Prom—were more important than me and the class I taught. Rather than resist these interruptions to the academic schedule, I had learned I was better off ceding the ground and leaning into the festivities. I had taken to wearing old "vintage" school shirts from my own days before big football games, analyzing lyrics from key songs during the musical's 'show week,' teaching boys how to tie half- and full-Windsor tie knots before homecoming, and demonstrating "ancient" eight- and ten-year-old dance moves before the Prom. Of all the annual traditions, the Dodge game was far and away the most important. Not only the cheerleaders and dance team, but all of the student organizations hung banners around the school, the student council organized a slate of "theme" dress-up days, and, in addition to the usual Friday afternoon pep rally before the game, there was a Thursday night bonfire attended by a large swath of the community. Music was played in the halls during passing periods, teachers were encouraged to join the students in dressing up for the theme days, and by Friday, a day the band marched through the halls before the beginning of the first class, the pitch of student excitement had been driven to such a fervor I would be better off showing slasher movies or slaughtering animals in my classroom than trying to teach.

It was fair of my students to expect, if not my full and active participation during this annual ritual, then at least my good-natured, open-handed looking the other way. But I found that parts inside of me that had formerly been flexible were now rigid, that my students' mirth and high-spiritedness were too much to bear. Faced with their twinkling-eyed roguishness and merriment—their *lassitude*—I felt my lips draw thin. I glowered at them, was short in my comments, and assigned extra homework. I raised my voice and yelled. I had, more than once in the course of the week, the awful feeling of having pulled the rug out from under my students and, before returning it, taken a shit in its center. It seemed by the middle of the week that not just the metaphorical atmosphere of my classroom, but also the physical space had become dimmer.

Then, on Thursday, I had the displeasure of hearing the click of heels and seeing our test-prep czar, Mrs. Hirsche, step into my darkened space.

My students were midway through a practice quiz—I had noted the beginning and ending times of their allowance on the board—and I stalked the aisles between their rows of desks emptily until it expired. They put their pencils down, and then I used my overhead projector to shine the correct answers on the board and go over right and wrong answers until she left. Likely, I had earned less than half of the box checks I usually accrued during a walk-through; possibly there would be a consequence for this. I watched my email for the rest of the day, though, and nothing came of it.

On Friday, a morning my students would have, any other year, been euphoric and rambunctious—full of piss and verve—my jock English class came in looking wan and meek. The timeworn mammalian commonplace they should have evoked was that of a bull in a china shop; instead they brought to mind a loyal old dog too often kicked. I knew I had broken their trust, that I should apologize, crack some jokes, ask them about their readiness—but I only lifted my stack of test-prep passages, three rotations-worth, and asked them to get out their paper, pencils, and pens.

Of the class's members, Javi was the hardest student to watch as we worked our way through these practices. The key to the class—a student not unlike Bryce, it occurred to me now—my relationship with him was the one I had worked the hardest in the course of the year to develop. In my state of dead-battery torpor, it was Javi I had most worried about bridling and leading the class in revolt against me. Instead, he had seemed to read my mood more quickly than his peers and match it by sinking into his own state of despondency. Now when he addressed me at the end of class it was with a voice so quiet that, had I not looked up, I would never have guessed its belonging to him.

"Hey Able," he said, his eyes large. "You gonna—I mean, are you coming to the game tonight, or what?"

In one of those moments a teacher can have, everything I knew about him from everything he had said and written and done in my class, from the introductory speech he had given to the personal reflections he had written to the jokes he had told and the tone he had told them in, came into my mind at once. That his dad was gone, his older brother, occasionally in trouble for either using or selling drugs, moved away, his sister married to a guy he didn't like. That he lived alone in a trailer with his "moms," singular, and despised the three men he was most closely related to but wasn't sure he wouldn't end up much like them. That I, in conjunction with some of the coaches on the team, had come to fill an important, lacking, male role in his life. That he had come, in some small ways, to depend on me.

All of this I intuited dimly, but didn't understand. The class was almost over—the bell about to ring—and he had taken me by surprise.

"I don't think so," I said. "I—"

"It's okay," he said, shaking his head in a manner that suggested the contrary. "You do you."

He turned at the same time the bell rang. I tried to call him back, but it was too late. He was gone.

OVER THE COURSE of the next several hours my understanding caught up with my intuition. I was important to Javi, to half the boys on my roster, really, beyond the simple fact that I taught them English lessons and entered their grades in the online grade book. What's more, I was an adult, while they were children. I had an obligation to them and might, I realized, benefit on a soul-level from fulfilling it. Outside it was a quintessential fall afternoon, neither cold nor warm but somewhere crisp and in-between. I understood that, as much as I wanted to, I wouldn't do myself any favors passing another weekend alone in my apartment, or going out to Kemper's or Oasis with Garret. A November football game, an away game in Dodge City with a meditative hour's worth of driving on either side, could be just the thing to break me out of my rut and maybe help me to get some traditionally scheduled sleep. And showing up unexpectedly—as a surprise—might be meaningful to Javi, Marcos, and my other guys on the team. It might warrant their forgiving me for how awful I'd been in the course of the week.

I decided to eat a sandwich and stay awake after school, leaving for Dodge sometime after five in order to arrive and be seen in the stands during the pregame warm-ups, but the pull of my couch and force of my recent habit proved too much to overcome. Lying down for what I thought might be a brief respite for my eyes—a fifteen-minute catnap—I awoke at half-past six, too late to make the drive to Dodge before the game's seven o'clock kickoff. I pulled on the same Plains City blue button-up I'd worn earlier in the day, anyway, sans necktie, swapped the slacks I had slept in for a pair of jeans, and flamingoed on a pair of brown loafers beside my front door. It was six-forty when I got into my car, forty-five after when I crossed over the dried-up Arkansas on the west bridge to get to the bypass, and ten 'til seven when Night Ranger's "Sister Christian" hit its chorus on my car radio just as I hit the onramp for highway 58, breaking free of Plains City's field of gravity. I switched on the radio and spun the dial until I found the game, just in time to hear Ted Matthews, the voice of the Chargers, finish announcing the starting lineups and listen to the Red Demon Marching Band's brassy interpretation of the national anthem.

The game, as described by Ted Matthews, began well enough for our side. Jeremy Ledesma received the kickoff in the middle of the end zone and ran it out to the thirty-two. Two runs and a pass play earned us two first downs and twenty-eight yards; a Red Demon offsides penalty netted us five more. A minute and thirty-eight seconds into the game and we had first and ten on Dodge's thirty-five yard line. Then things started to come apart.

Vinny Cruz, our starting center, came off the field for a play. Ryan Sellers, his sophomore replacement, muffed the hike, and Harrison Thompson, our senior quarterback, lost eight yards scrambling after he'd recovered the ball. Kade Wright was stuffed on his next two consecutive running attempts, and then a Dodge City player named Ricky Lathers picked off a pass attempt from Thompson to Jaime Delgado that Ted Matthews called both "rushed" and "ill-advised."

Dodge only needed three plays of their own to cover seventy yards and get into our end zone after that. When Ledesma dropped the next kickoff and Dodge's Silvares recovered, I reached forward to shut the radio off.

I could turn around. I was on pace to get to the game sometime late in the second quarter, anyway. It would be almost halftime by the time I had navigated the parking lot, the ticket entrance, and the visitor-side bleachers to find a seat. The way things were going the game could be out of hand by the beginning of the third quarter, and I might save my students some embarrassment if I wasn't there to watch. And if I turned around, I could be home by eight. I didn't want to pass another night out at the Plains City bars with Garret, but I could pick up take-out and rent a movie. It had been a while since I'd been to the rental place.

My headlights lit on a bright green sign. Dodge was

twenty-one miles ahead. Greensburg forty-eight. Wichita one hundred and one. "—brings the Chargers within eleven," said Ted Matthews when I switched the radio back on. "If the defense can get a stop on the next drive, here, we could really have a game to watch."

And we *did* get a stop. Archer, the Demon's Division-1 bound halfback, coughed up the ball as he tried to run through Carter Rios, our right tackle, and Marcos Dominguez came down on top of it. Harrison ran the ball himself on two of the next five plays, handed off to Kade twice for positive yardage, and then threw a screen pass to Quentin Early, who broke free and ran a third of the length of the field to bring the game within five. The extra point was good.

I sat up in my seat and cracked my neck. "Six minutes to go in the second. We could be watching something really special," Ted Matthews told his radio audience.

But we weren't watching something special. Or at least we Chargers fans weren't. Time seemed to slow as Dodge scored not once, not twice, but three times in the next three and a half minutes. Ted described the Plains City players as sitting down on their helmets, the coaches looking to the sky for answers—and there were still two minutes left in the nightmarish second quarter. I rolled past the gas stations, taco trucks, and Boot Hill Museum billboards on the outskirts of Dodge. Plains City went three and out and punted again, Dodge's Velasquez returning it fifty-two yards to the Plains City thirty-three. I turned the radio off and passed a stone-chiseled sign welcoming motorists to the Wild West. Just beyond it, a green sign announced that Greensburg was twenty-seven miles away, Wichita eighty. Davis popped into my mind. On Friday nights in college he'd often still be sleeping at this hour, getting ready for a big night out. Or we'd be out already, chicken wings and pitchers of beer for dinner, music he'd picked out and paid for with a half-roll of quarters playing on a juke box.

I had slowed to the city speed limit and was looking for a good place to turn around when a big, boxy ambulance came alive in a parking lot to my right, its lights flashing operating room white and prairie fire red. I pulled over to let it pass, and as it sped up I accelerated, too, until I was close enough behind to see the dents in its rear bumper and the angel's wing pattern where the EMTs' hands had brushed the dust away from its rear doors. I tailed it for the length of Wyatt Earp Boulevard and then we were heading out of town. *See Y'all Again Real Soon*, the sign said. "The hell out of Dodge," I muttered, something few but those of us who live in Western Kansas ever get to say and mean. Greensburg was twenty-three miles away; Wichita seventy-six. The ambulance slowed, wheeling off down a dirt road toward a farmer who'd suffered a stroke, or a rancher having a heart attack. There was something going on somewhere behind my own sternum; something growing and gathering momentum. I swerved around the ambulance as it turned, slingshotting beyond its brake lights, leaving both Dodge City and Plains City behind to go to Wichita, a place where I had a friend.

9

"Absolutely," Davis said after I'd pushed the button to speed-dial his number. Long gone was the desolate, broken Davis of the funeral. This was the big, boisterous voice that had called to ask about 'me' and 'I' six nights before; the commanding voice that had lead us on a hundred adventures in high school and college. "Come over. You remember where I used to be, right? I've got a new place. It's close to there." He gave me the directions. "We'll get you busted up. Get you laid, too." He laughed his huge laugh. "How soon do you think you can be here? I'll order some pizza. And you can meet Jules, too. You'll like her."

His new place was, as he'd explained, not far from his old one, in a complex with better landscaping and stone facades on the lower levels of the buildings. There was an immense, shining truck, a red F-250 with dealer tags on it, parked in front. As soon as the door was open, he clapped me in his linebacker's embrace. "Fucking Golden Boy," he said when he held me back out, using a nickname I hadn't heard or thought about in years. He pulled me back in. "You guys took good fucking care of me with that business back home. Good fucking care." I thought he might cry, then— there was a kind of a micro-shudder—but he was grinning, almost laughing when he let me go. He handed me a Corona with a wedge of lime pinched into the top and gestured toward a beige sectional couch I didn't recognize stationed in front of a flatscreen TV that looked new, too, a Friday night football game taking place between two college teams. There was a pizza box on the low table between them. "Eat up. I'm gonna take care of you tonight, Goldie."

The pizza was meat-laden and glistening; I didn't realize how hungry I'd been until I took a bite. Then I felt enlivened, as if grease were an essential dietary component I had been deprived of. When I lifted the bottle to wash my mouth with the cereal and lime of the Corona, I realized I had been thirsty without knowing it, too. I drank deeply, finishing half the bottle, and sank back into the couch to watch the game.

Davis called to me from the bathroom, but between the announcers' call and my chewing, I only partially heard what he had to say. "Play some pool... Jules... Dance place... Else we could..."

By the time he came out, his hair still wet and his cheeks ruddy, I had a third slice of pizza in hand and was midway through my second bottle of his Mexican beer.

"You about ready to go?" he asked, and I glanced with some misgiving at the televised game I both didn't care about and had begun to become invested in.

"Just about," I told him.

"Got this two weeks ago," Davis said of the truck parked in front of his apartment, and we more or less flew to the pool hall several blocks away, Davis cranking the stereo and stomping on the gas and brakes by turn as we approached and left behind stop signs and traffic lights. Shuttled from front to back and side to side in the passenger seat, I vaguely enjoyed my lack of control as his passenger. It reminded me of other car rides in high school and college when being first to call 'shotgun' had been a point of distinction and dips in the road had been approached with speed instead of caution.

Varsity, the pool hall, was cavernous, its front windows and the walls inside covered floor to ceiling with memorabilia and neon lights. Half a football field's worth of green felt stretched to a back wall that was hard to make out in the dimness of the place. Davis changed a twenty for two rolls of quarters and ordered a pitcher of beer, and we walked to a table in the middle of the floor.

"You look like you could stand to hit the gym," Davis said after we'd gotten five or six balls into a first game.

"I've been pretty busy," I said to explain myself.

He came around and pinched a tuft of the hair at my temple. "Maybe get a haircut and a little sun, too."

Davis's own hair was neatly trimmed, and he looked like *he* had been hitting the gym and getting some sun. The last time I'd seen him, at Bryce's funeral, he'd been a wreck, bloated by sadness, drunk from drinking with his dad all afternoon, well on his way to being passed out at our table at the Oasis before eleven o'clock.

"What would you be doing if I hadn't called you tonight," it occurred to me to ask.

He bent to line up a shot, sunk the solid yellow number five. "Probably watching the game," he said as the ball fell into the pocket. "Having Jules over a little later."

I nodded, looked him over with renewed curiosity. The beer he was drinking was still only his second I knew of for the night, and he wasn't rushing me to finish my own. He hadn't called me a 'bitch,' a 'little bitch,' or a 'pussy' yet in the course of the evening—had hardly dropped more than one or two f-bombs that I could recall. He seemed to be, rather than bombastic and bullying, as I remembered him, concerned, even solicitous. Could it be that my old friend Davis, whom I'd long lumped with Garret as a kind of arrested-adolescent man-child, the most aggressive and belligerent of my aggressive and belligerent old friends, was growing up? I caught my reflection in a Michelob Light logo-etched mirror on a pillar nearby. I did look pale, and if not outright thin, then at least a little gaunt. And I *was* past due for a haircut. If either of us looked arrested in adolescence, it was me, the one still passing his days in the high school we had each graduated from nearly eight years before.

"Hey Davis," a voice called, singing out the syllables of his name. When I turned, I saw a brunette in black jeans, tall, whose haircut and smile brought Monica from *Friends* to mind.

Davis offered her his easy grin. "Hey Theresa," he called back.

"Is that—" I started to ask, and Davis shook his head. "That's Theresa. My girl is *Jules*. Hey Mother Theresa, grab us another pitcher, a couple a shots?"

"Will do." She bobbed her head, seemed to add the order to a mental notepad.

He shot his chin in her direction after she'd turned to walk away. "She might be interested in you. We'll see where the night takes us."

I pivoted to watch her lean against the bar and put our order in. As unlikely as such a liaison seemed, the possibility of it—and the corresponding possibility the night might take another, similarly unlikely turn—gave me a charge. My pulse didn't quicken so much as leap, and I remembered this as another feature of being around Davis —the way he drew me out of my interior life of perhaps too much contemplation and thrust me into a physical world that was both unpredictable and frequently exhilarating. Now he began a hollered, obscene, sparring conversation with a group of leather-clad bikers a few tables away about a pop song he was accusing them of having chosen on the hall's juke box, and it occurred to me that I, too, might someday leave Plains City, take on a decent-paying job other than teaching, meet women in pool halls and bars on Friday nights, and exchange friendly barbs with motorcyclists.

"Tell me about this Jules," I said when he and the bikers had finished.

He turned to me and grinned. Jules, he said, had graduated from the same college as us and taught public school for a few years but was teaching private, now, at a Saint Somebody's. She coached girls soccer and track and—

And I knew her. She was walking in. Her hair was longer, and her features softer with a few years' maturity, but I would have recognized her even if Davis hadn't primed me to do so. Julia Lauer. We'd had classes together, English 311, 410, and 660, and had collaborated on a group presentation with a pair of classmates to present on the recurring motifs of stasis and self-deception in Joyce's *Dubliners*. Over the course of three weeks in the first semester of my junior year we had met on the second floor of the library, congregated around the pastry crumbs and coffee rings on tables at a late-night study spot called Waker's, and, one night, descended into the basement bar of Harold's, from which we emerged to go dancing at a club called The Pelican Bar.

Julia was from Wichita herself, I now remembered. It made sense that she and Davis had bumped into one another. Even in a city Wichita's size, their separate orbits must have overlapped at a number of points, and even if they hadn't, their separate gravities would inevitably have drawn them together.

It was comforting to see that she recognized me, too. "It's *so* good to see you," she said, her eyes wide, lips a little apart.

I let her know the feeling was mutual. There's an impulse for old friends to embrace, but we hadn't quite been friends—hadn't quite been anything. We might, in fact, have been best categorized as *not quites*. We had shared a rapport in college—I'd had a crush on her and would have asked her out, but she'd had a boyfriend at the time. It was too bad. Now I offered her my hand, and she took it. Hers was warm, dry, and soft. Mine was sorry to let it go.

"Oh!" she said, spinning back to Davis. "How'd your meeting go?"

To avoid the risk of having my sudden view of her backside burn into my retinas, I looked up to Davis, too. "You have a big meeting?"

"Dallas," she said, her hands finding purchase on his biceps as she slid to his side. "With the Rangers."

"The Texas Rangers? The baseball team?"

"He had a meeting with the *Texas Rangers*. The *baseball* team."

A few minutes' explanation—Julia did as much talking as he did—brought me up to speed. Davis had scored a big sale for MechaKleen, the company he had recently become the head salesman for. He had sold a dozen of the company's two-wheeled, gyroscopically-balanced janitorial vehicles to the athletic department at Wichita State down the road to clean the basketball team's Koch Arena after games. This had led to a pair of bigger sales—small fleets of the machines to Kansas State and the University of Kansas, where the two-wheeled models were augmented by back-pack-mounted vacuum cleaners and trash blowers for cleaning the rows of seats in their basketball arenas, and big, Zamboni-style floor cleaners for long concrete concourses of the football stadiums. Other MechaKleen products were being adopted for use by the universities' grounds crews, and word was spreading to other Big-12 schools, schools in the Big-10, and programs in the SEC. A meeting with the Royals hadn't panned out, but this one yesterday with the Rangers had. The Kansas City Chiefs and Dallas Cowboys were too deep in their seasons to commit to anything now, but each had agreed to meetings after their seasons ended. "Don't tell anyone," Davis said. "But I'm rooting against either of them going very far in the playoffs."

I felt myself go pale by degrees as they spoke. My friend wasn't just growing up—he was becoming successful. *Very* successful. Rich, even. The new furniture and television in his apartment, the shining new truck, the appliances on the counters in his kitchen—he'd even had a big, solid wood cutting board—flashed into my mind. Working for this company that, three years before, he hadn't been sure he would stick around with for more than six months. A company he hadn't been sure would *last* for six more months in its former aviation tool-shop, designing its bizarre cleaning contraptions. "Congratulations," I heard myself say, and his huge, meaty hand wrapped itself around my more modestly-sized one. Julia's hands crept further up his arm and I felt my earlier excitement at seeing her slip away, replaced by envy.

Davis gently unlaced his girlfriend's fingers from his bicep. "I gotta hit the head," he said. "You two catch up."

A foursome of stools was situated around a high-top table where Theresa had deposited our pitcher and glasses while Julia and Davis had caught me up on his recent successes. I sat down on one of these while Julia leaned over the back of another. "So how is it?" she asked after we'd situated ourselves. There was a 'just us now' intimacy about her question that I couldn't get a read on. Was she talking about our seeing one another again?

"How's what?" I asked.

She smiled, tilted her head. "How's teaching?"

Teaching. Her enthusiasm for the subject—the way she had her hands folded together over the stool-back as if ready to settle in for a long conversation—made it seem as if she'd been anticipating this intimate question about our shared profession since Davis had told her I was coming.

She leaned in. "You don't have any good stories to tell? Not one?"

It was her exactly as I remembered her—the inquisitive, invested way she'd had back in college, but sharpened. Teacherly. The way she posed her questions gave me an immediate sense of how she taught her classes. Hers was the kind of hopeful face a student wouldn't want to let down. I was sure her kids would go to the moon for her.

"There was a morning a while back when I caught the drumline coming in from their zero-hour marching practice," I said, embarking on the story of Dylan Bell and his friends following me, pied-piper-like, into the building. As I told it, a smile of approval came to her lips.

"Don't you love it?" She asked when I finished.

"Sometimes," I admitted.

"But not always?"

"I... Are you familiar with William Gramley? He wrote Stories Don't Matter in the Real World."

Her blank look told me she was not.

I hesitated, unsure I wanted risk letting the icy grip of

dread renew its grasp of my stomach. The look on Julia's face—sunny, almost entreating—compelled me to continue. "He's a teacher in California, on the cutting edge of pedagogical practice, supposedly. He's arguing against the use of traditional literature like novels and plays and poetry in the classroom. In favor of more nonfiction and short-passage stuff and test-prep instead. The admins in my district are big fans."

Hearing myself say this, the thing that had been, to borrow from Holden Caulfield, depressing the hell out of me, I felt foolish. In the air it sounded small and insignificant: too absurd to mention to someone as bright and buoyant as Julia Lauer on a Friday night. But some of the animation native to her face went out as I finished speaking. Her brightness dimmed and some of her buoyancy went out of her.

"No novels?"

"No novels."

"No plays?"

"No plays."

"And no poetry?"

"You get the sense they'd prefer poems didn't exist."

Some of her dismay was replaced by indignation. "So after all that, what's left? Writing?"

I shook my head. "They don't even want us teaching writing. They want short passages and multiple-choice work. All test-prep, all the time. For the tests."

"Because 'stories don't matter in the real world.'" Her brow wrinkled while perhaps fifteen or twenty seconds passed, then smoothed out. "That's stupid," she said decisively. "Stories matter to *me*." She gestured toward the table of bikers Davis had been jawing with. "They matter to those guys." She looked off toward the front of the bar, where

Theresa and a little five-foot-tall, blonde waitress were talking to the bartender and Davis. "They matter to them." She looked at me. "And they matter to you, don't they?"

I found that my mouth had gone dry. "Very much," I croaked.

"Not teach Gatsby or Romeo and Juliet, or To Kill a Mockingbird or Fahrenheit? That seems stupid. I'm doing Romeo and Juliet right now with my freshmen. Do you do Romeo? I love it. My students love it."

Her brightness came back, and her buoyancy brought her up from the submerged place she had only briefly visited. She was speaking now about Romeo and Benvolio, Mercutio and Tybalt, and Juliet and the friar as if they were friends we had gone to college with. As she spoke, I felt my stomach untwist and my spine relax. The tangle of vasculature surrounding my heart and lungs that had begun to thicken, tighten, and calcify in place came loose, and I found myself sitting up straighter, breathing more easily.

Davis came back with a tray of shots and told us he'd spoken to Theresa and one of her friends, the little blonde one. "Good news," he said as he set the tray down. "Mother Theresa and her friend Sam are going to the Club Annabelle with us after they finish their closing duties."

10

W e took our shots and the night washed along. Davis and I played two more games of pool while Julia looked on, then we teamed up to play a pair of two-on-twos with the bikers. Another pitcher of beer arrived, and then another. We waved goodbye to Theresa and Sam, who promised to complete their closing duties and see us as soon as they could leave. Then there was the chirp and flash of Davis remotely unlocking his new truck, the memorized lyrics and basslines of old nineties rap songs playing on his stereo, and we were careening around corners and speeding under streetlights on our way to the Club Annabelle.

Davis waved to the bartender and ordered our first round of drinks after we were inside—dark caramel-colored and cough-syrupy for him and me, clear and fizzing with a cherry bobbing atop its ice for Julia—and then he was hunkering down over his phone at a table and shooing us toward the dance floor.

"What's he—" I began to ask, elevating my voice above

the thrum, and "He doesn't think there are enough people here. He's calling some more!" Julia shouted in return.

We stepped onto a black and white checkered dance floor bound on two sides by a wrought iron railing and entered a new, late phase of the night's dreamlike trajectory. I felt as if a pair of my life's timelines had been severed, swapped, and spliced; that I had skipped from one in which I had accidentally become a high school teacher in my hometown to one in which I had taken a job in a bigger, more urban area where I went out with girls like Julia on the weekend. In this new, more appropriate timeline, I felt a renewed sense of some of the lightness and ease I remembered having possessed a scant few years before. The age of twenty-six, which had recently felt deathly old, seemed young again, like sixteen, nineteen, or twenty-two.

On the dance floor, with its mixed bouquet of sweat and rum-based drinks, our shadows flashing against the brick wall, I couldn't help but recall the night Julia and I had danced like this at the Pelican Bar. Julia's shoulder dip and shimmy were the same, as was the way she threw her head back to sing with the onset of any chorus. Dancing came back to me, and I remembered there'd been a time I was thought to be good at it. Backing inadvertently into a barrier at the edge of the floor and dropping my hand to steady myself, I was surprised to find the cool, wrought iron of the Annabelle's railing in my hand and not the smooth, painted two-by-four I had known at The Pelican. We danced for two songs, then three, an appropriate, this-is-my-friend's-girlfriend distance between us, then headed back to the table to check up on Davis.

"Any luck?"

"Some."

The way he squinted and looked out across the bar

made it clear Davis still found the present crowd woefully inadequate. There were new drinks on the table, two low cups for Davis and me and another tall glass with a cherry balanced atop for Julia. She drank off two-thirds of hers through a straw and met my eyes from across the table. "Dance?"

I looked to my friend. "You coming?"

"Give me a little bit." He raised his hand and motioned us away in the manner of a man tossing a beach ball into a crowd.

No more than five or six minutes could have passed, but the dance floor had become much more closely packed since Julia and I had stepped away. Her hand took mine as we crossed from the red tile of the bar's main space to the checkered space reserved for dancing, and she pulled me toward the naked brick wall at the Annabelle's rear. In the crush of bare skin and flashing of lights near the DJ's booth I could smell not only the vodka, cherry, and lime on her breath, but also her Clinique perfume, Dove body soap, and tang of sweat. The message suddenly—finally—became clear. Julia and I were better suited for one another than she and Davis. As students who shared Serendipity as a guidance counselor, we had not only English, but also History and Chemistry together. Davis was backing off—he was going to pursue Theresa, or Sam, or someone else, someone I didn't know of. There could be tens, even hundreds of phone numbers for attractive, available women in a phone like Davis's. He was ceding Julia to me.

The music was loud, the lyrics more imperative than suggestive. Not for the first time in my life, not for the first time dancing with this particular partner, I wondered how a thoughtful, articulate woman could not only tolerate lyrics instructing her to bend over and touch her toes, but follow them. My hands were on her hips, then her sides, then slipping around to her back where her shirt was damp beneath her lowest ribs.

I had a moment of doubt, then. The possibility that I had misconstrued everything came to me, and I took a half-step back. "I'm sorry," I said. I showed her the palms of my hands.

She tilted her head to regard me for a beat, then threw her chin back to laugh, the cathedral's dome at the top of her mouth illuminated by the stained glass of the bar's flashing lights. She reached up to press her palms to mine, brought my hands back down to her sides. Rising up on her toes, she spoke beside my ear. "Good Pilgrim," she said. "You wrong your hands too much."

When Davis finally joined us, he had Theresa and Sam in tow. As he'd formerly done in college, he became a monolithic presence on the dance floor: a deep-nodding, arms-in-the-air idol. The crowd that had pressed in around Julia and I spread out to give him room. He had too much girth now to move his feet much, but he had mobile hips and loved shouting along with song lyrics. Julia danced a few circles around him when he arrived, the pool hall waitresses moving to my either side, and then Theresa and Sam were dancing on either side of Julia. Davis took the hand of a sapphic, pierce-laden girl with orange, ringleted hair who I wasn't sure had been a part of our party, but might have just become one, and then the configurations changed again, everyone moving.

The style of dance that was most popular at the time, the one we'd had to break up and forbid at the high school dances, but which the students in the center of the dance floor always partook of, anyway, involved the female turning away from her male counterpart and bending over in front of him. She backed up, then—or he took hold of her and pulled her back—and ground her posterior against his groin in time with the music. A standing lap dance, basically. Doggy-style dry-humping. It was little Sam who turned and bent over before me first, not even quite tall enough to fully execute the maneuver. Then Julia slipped into her place almost as soon as the tiny blonde had vacated it. It was embarrassing, really. I looked around instinctively to see if anyone I knew was watching, but I was in Wichita, not Plains City, and the only people I saw nearby were strangers in similar postures to my own. Theresa was bent over with her hands on her knees in front of my friend tossing her hair in time with the music. Davis caught my eye and held it for a moment. When I raised my eyebrows, he raised his hands, joining his forefingers and thumbs to give me a double A-Ok sign, a gesture he augmented with his deep-nodding approval.

WE LEFT the dance floor to have another round of drinks, and returned for more dancing. I wasn't sure if we'd made new friends in the course of the last hour or if a number of Davis's existing friends had responded to his text messages and shown up, but it seemed that almost everyone there had become a part of our party. Then it was last call, and the lights were coming up, and everyone was being asked to leave, the black-shirted bouncers holding their brooms sideways like cattle pushers to guide us out. Back in Davis's truck I let my right arm trail lazily outside the window and rested the palm of my left on Julia's leg. Davis blared several more of our old anthems on his stereo as the traffic lights gave way before us, and then we were back at his place eating what was left of the pizza and filling glasses of water from the tap. Was anyone else coming over? No. Did I want another beer? I thanked him, anyway.

Julia stepped forward, her eyes shining, and grasped my hands in her own. "Good pilgrim, it was so good to see you tonight," she said. She kissed me on the cheek and disappeared into the bedroom.

Davis pulled a blanket from his closet, an old Afghan I recognized as technically belonging to me, by way of my mother, that we'd used to keep on the couch in our house in college. He tossed it over to me. He pointed to the TV remote on the end table and told me I could watch some, if I wanted, and then said goodnight. In the dark, the vertical blinds hanging down before the sliding door swung on air currents generated by the overhead fan. The corresponding, irregular sway of the shadows from the outside floodlights against the walls gave the room the feel of a ship tipping back and forth on an uneven sea. There was something I had missed in the course of the night; something I had misunderstood. The couch I was on shared a wall with Davis's room. The worst part of everything, worse than my short-lived hopes and expectations coming to naught, worse than my inability to understand how I had misread everything so thoroughly, was the fact I could hear the two of them through the wall.

11

I woke before the sun was much in the sky the next morning, put on my shoes, and snuck out of Davis's apartment without waking either of my friends. Stopping at the first pair of golden arches I came across, I bolted two breakfast burritos, a hotcake and sausage tray, and a plastic cup of orange juice, taking a Styrofoam cup of coffee to go, learning from the sports section of an abandoned copy of the Wichita Eagle that my Chargers had ultimately fallen to the Red Demons by a score of fifty-six to seventeen. According to the breakdown in the box scores, we had scored ten of our points in the last quarter. I took this to mean Dodge had started putting in their junior varsity players at the end of the game.

I filled my car with gas at a station next door to the McDonald's, bought a banana and a liter-sized bottle of water inside, and set out to leave Wichita.

Good Pilgrim, you wrong your hands too much.

Had I *not* wronged my hands? It had been a while since I'd taught *Romeo and Juliet.* Which scene in Act I or II was that from?

Reflecting upon the events of the evening in the light of day, with protein and sugar and caffeine fresh in my bloodstream, the last of the night's alcohol burning away, I wondered how I could have misunderstood things so badly. Had I been that drunk? Was I so desperate and lonely as to have willfully misconstrued the situation? The more I thought about it, the less I was sure my hopes had been unreasonable. Hadn't Julia and I had a connection? Didn't she and I make sense together? More sense than she and Davis? And couldn't he have taken home any number of girls—two at the very least—who made more sense with him than Julia did?

I spent much of the drive back to Plains debating these questions. On Wichita's outskirts I was almost too ashamed to reflect on what a fool I'd been to rest my hand on Julia's thigh during the drive back to Davis's apartment; by the time I reached Kingman I had inventoried Davis's personality and compared it to my own to prove that Julia and I made more sense than she and he; from this conclusion it was the small, bitter leap (and the short drive to Pratt) to the conclusion that when a girl is as attractive as Julia there comes to be a threshold in terms of the quality of a guy's personality. After we suitors pass it, we're all pretty much the same and what comes to matter most is how much money we make. By the time I reached Greensburg the degree to which this line of reasoning was unfair—and abhorrent—had settled on me, and I descended the emotional ladder I had been moving up and down, again, down, down, down until I again reached my rock-bottom basement of shame and embarrassment.

～

PULLING BACK into Plains City and letting myself into my apartment just before noon, I fixed myself a quick lunch and retrieved my heavy green Norton compilation of Shakespeare's works from my shelf. The line Julia had quoted was in Act I, scene v. The lovers had just met, and this was the famous exchange about fingers and lips—how lips ought to do what fingers did. A note in the text suggested Romeo was dressed as a pilgrim, but admitted to an aura of ambiguity. If Shakespeare had anticipated the evening I was destined to have five hundred years later (which is what I'd half come to believe), then *pilgrim*, with its benign, impotent connotations and associations with elementary school students in hats of construction paper, seemed appropriate.

I showered, and when I returned to my bedroom found that my cell phone was ringing. *Davis,* the readout said, but when I answered, the voice on the other end of the line was Julia's.

"Hey, do you have a copy of that book we were talking about last night?" she asked.

"Romeo and Juliet?" I asked, stupidly.

"No. Stories Don't Matter in the Real World. I dragged Davis to the bookstore at the mall and we're here looking at it. Have you read it?"

I told her that I had it, but hadn't begun reading it yet.

"Do you have it handy? Go get it. Go to page... one hundred seventy-seven."

I did as I was told, retrieving the Gramley text from my shelf and leafing through the pages.

"It's the second page of the last chapter. Read the first sentence of the first new paragraph."

I read.

While I believe heartily in preparing students for academic and professional communication, and know that research writing is a skill that pays dividends in many more ways than our students may ever realize, I've come to believe that teaching Shakespeare—yes, that Shakespeare, the bard—should be the ultimate goal of all high school English and Language Arts curricula. My reasons for elevating the bard—for reaffirming the bard's already established position at the top of the hierarchy— are as follows...

"Huh," I said.

"The whole book is like that. He's not *in favor* of removing books from classrooms to teach test-prep. He's *opposed* to it."

I flipped back through the book's pages, glancing at its diagrams, in-set text boxes, and chapter titles until I finally reached the introduction at the beginning. "Huh," I said again.

"Anyway, I thought you should know. It looks like its pretty good. I'm going to make Davis buy me a copy. Hey, speaking of, he wants to talk to you."

I heard the muffled sound of the phone being handed off. "What the fuck?" my friend said. "We were going to take you out to brunch."

"Sorry."

"No worries. You got home alright? Not too hungover? I caught a *fierce* one...."

I told him I'd gotten home alright; that I, too had had a bad hangover.

"We'll do it again. Maybe next time get here sooner so we can get in a real meal first. Set you up with one of Julia's teacher friends, maybe."

I agreed that this all sounded good, and we clicked off. I looked down and began reading the introduction to Gramley's book:

Eighth period English. Eighteen boys and eleven girls. English for the indifferent: shop kids, metal kids, motor heads, and burnouts. In my first year of teaching, this class would be my crucible. Here I would learn whether I had what it took to teach, or if I was, as I secretly feared, a mere mortal. Every day was a battle. My students' chief weapons were their indolence and apathy; their strategy to erode my expectations. They wanted to bring things to a head every class; to say "We can't!" and then prove it. But I never let them give up. I coaxed them into turning in quarter-finished and half-finished assignments, turn-ins that I saw in the moment as victories, but looked back on later as defeats.

It wasn't until my third year (I was already partially resigned, already just going through the motions in mid-October after another year's inauspicious beginning) that one of my students, a senior, piped up and said something that shook me—shook me like a cataclysm—and jarred loose the frozen slurry that had taken hold and begun to solidify at my core. What he said, was, "Mr. Gramley, why are we doing this? You know stories don't matter in the real world, right?" and when I said, "Oh, but they do matter, Anthony, they really do," it wasn't him who was unalterably changed by the answer I gave, but me.

I felt my vision begin to cloud, and I looked up from the text.

"She didn't even read it," I said. She had seen the title and heard something about it—maybe read the table of contents—but Mrs. Hirsche *hadn't read the book*. I stood and looked at my bookshelves. The Head of Literacy hadn't read Gramley's book, and the curriculum she was building was based on the title of the book she hadn't read. Then I laughed, because the book she hadn't read was *opposed* to everything she was doing. Because the title was *ironic* and she, the *Head of Literacy*, didn't know it—and that in itself was ironic. I sat down on my couch and I laughed, and I clutched the book and I laughed, and I pounded the cushion and I laughed, and I laughed and I laughed— because if it wasn't funny, it was just fucking sad, wasn't it?

12

"Sorry I didn't make it to your game," I said to Javi when he arrived at my classroom door on Monday morning.

He had trudged down the hall with decidedly less bounce in his step than I had seen him arrive with heretofore. No bounce, in fact. "It's alright. We got wasted."

I stepped across his path. "No. I should have been there. Six catches for 72 yards isn't bad against a lockdown defense. Who do you guys have this weekend? Hays?"

"Yeah, Hays." He looked up.

"I'll be there." I stepped back out of his way. "Make sure you guys have a good week of practice. Getting knocked down isn't what matters, getting back up is."

Class began and I had my students get out their notebooks.

"We not doing the packets?" Marcos asked.

"I thought we'd start a new unit today. I thought we'd start it with some writing."

Marcos nodded, enough a show of approval to speak for

the rest of the class, most of whom were already rummaging in their bags.

"Are you guys individuals or conformists?" I asked. "That is, do you do your own thing, or do you mostly follow along and live up to other people's expectations? I assume a lot of you want to try to argue both ways, but you can't. You have to figure which way you tilt, then start your essay with 'I am a *blank*,' and then offer two or three examples. I'm looking for about a page-front. I'll write all of these instructions on the board—if you're ready, you can start writing now."

The Individual and Society was the title of the next unit in the old curriculum after *The Writings & Rhetoric of the American Revolution*. It addressed the American Romantic movement of the early 1800s. With its emphasis on poetry and the often-difficult writings of Emerson ("Self-Reliance") and Thoreau ("Civil Disobedience"), it was one of the units most often cited by the Central Office administration as unnecessary and counter-productive in the English classroom. Because it enabled me to ask questions such as *Are you guys individuals or conformists?*, and because it addressed big-idea topics such as our place in nature, the tensions between our private lives and our civic ones, and the various roles institutions play in our lives, I'd long thought it might be the most important unit I taught.

I spent my morning and afternoon classes introducing the unit to my juniors, and after school stopped at Wonder's to pick up coffee and a cherry-filled doughnut. This was the second part of the plan I had devised over the weekend: I thought some sugar and a good dose of caffeine might get me through the afternoon, and that I thus might start to break the vicious cycle of my napping habit.

I ate half of my pastry before reaching the door of my apartment and found, after I'd let myself in, that the power of habit was stronger than I'd expected. Merely walking across my threshold induced me to yawn, and even after I'd opened and raised all of the apartment's blinds and turned on all of the lamps and overhead lights in my living room there wasn't enough light to ensure my staying awake for the next hour, much less four or five. If I sat down on my couch or the floor, I was sure I would nod off.

So I ate the rest of my doughnut and turned around with my coffee, leaving my apartment to walk up and down Main Street and around the nearby neighborhoods for the next hour and a half. I found, when I returned, that if I had managed to keep myself awake, I had also worn myself further out, and when I regarded my couch, I did so warily. I could get more coffee, I thought, but might run the risk of exceeding the other mandate I'd set for myself: I wanted *not* to nap after school, but also wanted to be able to fall asleep sometime before midnight and sleep through the night. If I failed in this, I would almost certainly find myself in a similar situation tomorrow. I decided I ought to leave my apartment again, this time to eat dinner at the bar at Dos Amigos.

I walked again after dinner, for another hour, and it was after eight when I returned to my apartment, sure that I couldn't walk anymore and not sure falling asleep now would be such a bad idea. I took a shower and found that it reinvigorated me—this, or that my present circadian rhythms were wired to cycle to 'high' just before nine. My couch now looked like a place where I might sit wide-awake for the next six hours—where I might watch red-enveloped DVDs and television into the wee hours, perhaps popping popcorn, or ordering a pizza around midnight. I couldn't turn on the television, I decided. The thing to do was sit down and *read*. The situation called for something entertaining but challenging; something that would keep me engaged, but also wear me out. My eyes fell on the heavy green compilation I had pulled down two days before. I would read some Shakespeare, I decided. I lifted the tome and flipped to the table of contents. *King Lear* seemed appropriate for a November night. I sat down and began to read.

MY FATHER TOLD me he had a question for me, and I agreed to have dinner with him that Friday night. Over wide bowls of pho and thin strips of grilled pork and vegetables on cracked rice I prepared for him to ask me whether I was ready to head off to law school yet—or if I was trying to destroy the family name with my antics working for the school district—but neither of these questions came up. Instead, while we waited for our iced coffees to arrive for dessert, he brought up Sharon Rhodes.

"I'd like to take Sharon to Mexico for the week of Christmas," he said. "It would be over your winter break. Would you be willing to watch the house and dogs for me?"

I said I would, of course.

"The freezer will have steaks in it and the fridge will be stocked. I'll make sure my subscriptions are up to date— you'll be able to catch the holiday tournaments and bowl games."

If I did decide to get away, he said—if I was going to visit my mother or get out of town with some friends—Sharon's daughter Bethany could be contacted to step in and take care of things.

"I'll do it," I told him. "Happy to."

My father picked up the check. The sun was setting

before either of us had walked in, and the night had matured from twilight to darkness while we ate. Getting into my car and pulling out of my spot onto the street, I felt a kind of restlessness for an evening I hadn't felt in Plains City since I didn't know when. After my evening the last Friday night in Wichita with Davis and Julia—and my last several nights of walking and reading—staying in seemed unfathomable. Turning left instead of right to leave the lot, I drove toward Garret's.

I TAUGHT my unit on the Romantics over the next several weeks, shrugging off the administrative walk-throughs that came through my door and earning myself a second Form-57 for the year, and I stopped by Wonder's each afternoon for a coffee and one of their many various pastries after school. The 'hard break' that had formerly existed between my daytime and nighttime existences smoothed out, and I finished reading *Lear,* then took up *Much Ado about Nothing.* Finishing *Much Ado,* I took up *Macbeth*, and finishing *Macbeth*, I began *Twelfth Night*, reading an act or two of each play each night before bed. Driving to Kansas City on the Wednesday before Thanksgiving, I passed the long weekend with my mother and grandmother. Borrowing a copy of *Emma* from my grandmother's considerable library, I began to mix a chapter or two of Austen's classic into my evening reading schedule, as well. Before the beginning of finals week, my "grinding" issue seemed to have resolved itself, and I retired my dental appliance to a shelf in my closet.

I taught a brief research writing unit in December and cobbled together a kind of 'greatest hits' of the off-curriculum readings I had taught in the course of the semester—including some Dickinson, Whitman, Twain, Emerson, and Thoreau—for my final.

"I thought you had better sense than this," Mrs. Hirsche said on the last day of the semester after she found me administering it.

"It's multiple-choice," I said in response. "I thought about making the entire thing short answer and essay, but I didn't want to spend my entire break grading."

She sighed and told me she would have to write me up. This, I told her, was no less than I had expected.

13

There was snow on the ground outside Wonder's, and particolored Christmas lights rimming the big plate glass windows inside. I was reading the copy of *Emma* I had borrowed from my grandmother's a month before, a cup of coffee and a buttered cinnamon twist on the table before me.

"I bet there's not another man within a hundred and fifty miles reading Austen right now," a voice said.

I closed the book and laid my hand over its cover as if to protect the author's ears. "Only a hundred and fifty?"

"Maybe farther."

I looked up and saw the face of a woman who looked to be in her early twenties. She had shoulder-lengthed blonde hair and was wearing a long, open camelhair coat and a creme-colored sweater. Her eyebrows rose as if in anticipation of a penny dropping, but on my end, the coin wouldn't fall. I recognized her, but couldn't tell from where.

"I'll give you a minute."

I scrutinized her, shook my head. "I'm not sure that's going to do it."

"My brother would be disappointed." She tilted her head. "Or, maybe not."

Then I had her—partially. "Matthew..."

Appliance-whitened teeth flashed between red-lipsticked lips. "That's *his* name."

"You'll be working for my father?"

"That's not my name."

"Pomerantz."

"Closer..."

"Kelsey. I'm not sure we've ever been properly introduced." I stood and held out my hand, but she leaned in past it, hugging me briefly like an old friend before stepping backward.

"I don't think that's true. It's just been eight or ten years."

"I might have been a senior," I suggested.

"You *were* a senior." Her lips parted to reintroduce her dazzling white teeth.

She had me flat-footed, and I wasn't sure what to do with the flirtation I heard in her voice. There was something in the intensity of her gaze, too, that was almost gleeful, as if she'd told a joke a few moments ago and was still waiting for me to catch up and get it so we could both start laughing. I found something in my chest leaping up to respond to her in an almost animalistic way. "You're in town for Christmas?"

"All the way through New Years."

"You'll have to give me your number so I can show you around."

Some of the laughter that had been threatening spilled over. "I *grew up* here."

"You still seem like someone who needs the guided tour." I handed her my phone.

She was obliged to spend some time with her parents in

the next couple nights, she said, but suggested I might see her the evening of the 23rd. A bunch of people were getting together at the Brush Bar, on the first floor of the country club. I could meet her there.

"I'm going to be out at my dad's, anyway. I'll see you then," I said.

The girl working the counter called out Kelsey's name. "I'll look forward to it," she said.

I PACKED a few things into a duffel bag that afternoon and drove out to my father's to let his dogs out and begin my stay housesitting.

Without being gaudy or ostentatious, the house my father had built on the rise at the end of Cottonwood Lane was widely considered to be among the most enviable on the country club's grounds. It overlooked the fourth hole's putting green to the south, and its elevation afforded it a better view of the course than any other dwelling ringing the greens. To the east, it boasted an unobstructed view of the Hackshaw Buffalo Preserve. Most mornings, at least some part of the herd was within view of his bedroom window. These qualities were nice, but the thing I found most appealing about my father's house in my first hours there was that it was *quiet*. After I'd finished my breakfast of steel-cut oats from his pantry and sausage patties and fresh berries from his refrigerator, I couldn't tell if it was the absence of the usual noise of my apartment or being free of my usual obligations and routines that gave me ability to *think*. And when I did think, I thought that this was perhaps a life that could be mine, quiet enough to allow for thought, with high ceilings and comfortable furniture and views of a putting green, a pond, a tin windmill, and a buffalo herd. I had, growing up, told myself a thousand times that I didn't need money like my father's to be happy. Drinking a cup of coffee I had made in his Italian coffee maker from a bag of beans he had mail-ordered in, padding around half-dressed in my father's comfortable home despite the low-twenties temperature outside, I found myself reluctantly admitting that only someone who'd had it so good as I had growing up could have made such a claim.

I let the dogs out, let them back in, refreshed their food and water, and then Harold and Winston settled into their beds on either side of my father's favorite chair. I spent some time looking over my father's books, and finally made my way to his home office, the desk of which he kept immaculately barren, to begin my work.

A number of things had become clear to me after my trip to Wichita and subsequent weeks of teaching Emerson, Thoreau, and the American Romantics. One of them was that I had, at some point in the previous three years, stopped actively pursuing my own life—that I had taken the car out of drive, shifted it into neutral, and coasted to a near-stop. Another was that I had allowed myself, perhaps as some kind of protective or defensive mechanism, to become entirely too invested in my teaching. Focusing on the daily problems of my classroom and the bigger-picture issues with the administration had distracted me from what I should have been worried about: my future. After I recognized these problems, the correct course of action to amend the situation became immediately clear: I needed to send off applications to continue my education. That I still wasn't sure whether I wanted to apply to law school or a graduate program in English I now recognized as a barrier that needn't have been as significant as I had let it become. I could apply to both, a handful of each, and make my decision in a few months based on what responses I received.

So I passed my morning outlining essays and drafting responses to short-answer questions, phoned-in and picked-up an order for lunch from the clubhouse's kitchen, and wrote the first drafts of several of the essays my applications required after eating my Jalapeño burger, fries, and pickle spear. Writing essays had never been a weakness for me—I had always earned good grades for my writing—but writing had always been painful, a late-night process. In high school and college, I had agonized over my authorial choices. Now, three-and-a-half-years of teaching behind me, I had an answer for every dilemma that arose, and a workaround for each roadblock. I worked quickly and methodically, dispatching four solid drafts before the time came for dinner. I grilled one of the steaks my father had left for me and watched part of a college basketball tournament on my father's satellite to pass the evening. At eleven, after I had let the dogs out and back in again, I finished two more chapters of *Emma* and went to bed.

The next day I was more productive in the morning and less-so in the afternoon. I walked the dogs after lunch and then fell to napping. After my dinner I thought that sitting down to look over the work I had done during the day might put me in a better place to improve my writing the next morning, and looking over a few of my essays turned into typing a few more paragraphs, and at the end of an hour I was so deeply in a groove I worried that if I climbed out to go meet Kelsey Pomerantz at the Brush Bar I wouldn't be able to climb back in. Surely she hadn't *really* been interested in meeting me—surely her invitation was merely polite. I had said I would go, though, and she would be working with my father in the summer. Much as I didn't think I should be, I felt constrained by filial obligations. Thinking I might have a drink and put in an hour's face time before coming back home, I saved my files and stood to dress and go out.

At the clubhouse I found a tableau I had once been intimately familiar with: twenty or thirty well-to-do graduates of PCHS dressed in their preppie best back for Christmas break charging drinks on their parents' club accounts. There was a quality of déjà vu about the display, made strange by the fact I only vaguely recognized anyone participating. The oldest of those I saw spread out before me had probably been sophomores when I graduated. I spotted Kelsey from the point where I had stopped beside the coat rack inside the bar's double doors, and her attitude, laughing between two of the tallest and preppiest-looking young men in the room, seemed to confirm the suspicion I'd had forty-five minutes earlier: that she'd been merely being polite when she saw me at Wonder's, and that my presence here was entirely unnecessary. The fact that I was too old for the crowd became pointedly clear before I had pulled my arms from my jacket's sleeves, and I was in the process of shrugging it back on when the taller of Kelsey's tall suiters called out "*Hey, Danny Zuko,*" across the bar. Partially because of the half-jacketed pose I was in, but also because of a dance routine I had participated in during a pep assembly my senior year, I knew he was speaking to me.

Kelsey was motioning for me when I looked back up, and, after a moment's hesitation, I reversed my action, stripping off my jacket to hang it with the others.

"I wasn't sure you were going to make it," Kelsey said after I'd joined them.

"Beer you?" asked the guy who had called me 'Zuko.'

I said *Sure,* and told them I could stick around for one.

The name "Layton" sprang into my mind. I remembered him, vaguely, as a freshman football running back who had played up to JV. His father was a dentist, or orthodontist. One of the ones no one in my family went to. He held his finger up for the bartender, and I could see that by this gesture he meant to show both his magnanimity and indifference to me—that he was working his charms on Kelsey Pomerantz and felt he had things pretty well locked-up. By the way their bodies were oriented, forming a sharp angle that only just allowed my own entrance into their conversation, it looked as if the two of them passing the rest of the night together might be a foregone conclusion.

"Just one?" Kelsey asked, turning toward me.

"I'm an old man now. I've only got room for one. I need to get home soon to watch some TV and go to bed."

I meant this only to signal my lack of intention—to extricate myself from the bar gracefully—but Kelsey seemed to take my exit plan up as an invitation. "Watch TV? That's what I need to do. Should we leave in, what, maybe an hour?"

Our drinks showed up and Layton signed for them, pivoting to set mine down in front of me more firmly than was necessary. Over the course of the next half hour, the smaller points of light around us, those shining down on bottles and glinting off the edges of our glassware, took on warmer and fuzzier glows as the bar became more crowded and the space between Kelsey and I narrowed. "Should we get out of here?" she asked sooner than I had expected.

"And go where?"

She squeezed my arm and looked up at me in a simpering kind of way. "Your place, silly. To watch television."

I agreed that we should. The glance I caught from

Layton on the way out made me think I would do well to avoid bumping into him anywhere else for the rest of the break.

Outside, the constellation of warm, fuzzy brightnesses within the Brush Bar seemed to have broken free of the bar's confines and been mapped onto the exterior world: landscaping lights shining up on the clubhouse, headlights of other arriving and departing cars, dash lights in my own car, illuminated windows of the condos that we passed.

"Shoes off?" Kelsey asked inside my father's front door, and "Do these seats recline?" after she had taken a seat on the sectional couch in the basement.

"It might take me a while to figure this out," I said, gesturing toward the trio of remotes lined up on the coffee table.

"That's okay," she said, pulling down the blanket draped over the couch's back. "Come over and do it from here."

14

We spent the better part of the next few hours that night running our hands over one another. When one o'clock neared, Kelsey abruptly rose, smoothed out her clothes, and announced she needed to go home. "Did I—" I began, but she shook her head.

"I have a curfew when I stay with my parents." She touched her chin, which was red, and stole close to kiss me again, her eyes filling back up with their laughter as she backed away. "Should we do this again?"

"Tomorrow?"

We met at the Brush Bar again at nine o'clock the next night, and were back at my father's before half-past ten. I had worked on my applications throughout the morning and afternoon, composing three new essays and polishing three of those I had already drafted, and when Kelsey and I wrapped ourselves together under the blanket on the couch that evening to watch a movie and begin working our fingers under the boundaries of one another's clothes, I felt hardworking, honest, and virtuous—a day laborer who'd put in his day's labor and returned home to his just reward. "How's law school," I asked over the rim of a glass of water during our first intermission.

Her face took on a pained expression. "I was so stressed out by the end of the semester I had to go to student health and get set up on Xanax." She set her glass down and slipped back in close to me. "I don't want to talk about it."

We stood up and went to my bedroom—the guest bedroom I was staying in—shortly thereafter.

"Can we just do hand stuff?" she asked, and I said *Sure*, that hand stuff was fine by me, and it was. Kelsey seemed to relish it—both the receipt and the giving of. After fifteen minutes of necking and my successful left-handed manipulations of her, she spent perhaps a quarter of an hour tipping me back and forth. She laughed uproariously when she brought me off.

That was Christmas Eve. I spent Christmas day on my own, filling out answers to demographic and short-answer questions for my applications, and passed the evening printing off and proofreading several of the essays I had written. The next day my father and Sharon came home and they—by which I mostly mean Sharon—urged me to stay at my father's for the next several days through the New Year so that we could enjoy the holiday together. I agreed, and the remainder of the year took on an altered tenor: no longer was I a sophisticated bachelor, Bruce Wayne alone haunting his manor; instead I was a teenager in my parents' basement, subject to their schedules and dictates. Which wasn't necessarily all bad: the food was good, as evidenced by that night's ham, scalloped potatoes, and fennel and orange salad.

We exchanged gifts on the morning of the twenty-seventh. I gave books by David McCullough and Janet

Evanovich to my father and Sharon (I had spun into town to get them the day before, my father having advised me on the latter purchase) and received a fancy German electric razor from my father and a book whose title and author I didn't recognize from Sharon. "It's about this oddball college professor," she explained, struggling to keep the caged birds of her hands from fluttering to her shoulders and face. "He teaches English at a college and gets into all these hijinks. I couldn't help but think of you when I read it."

I opened the book's cover and looked at the middle-aged man posed for his author photo on the inside of the flap. I typically didn't like books other people picked out for me, but this choice seemed thoughtful and didn't look too bad. Plus, I was on the verge of finishing my Austen novel and hadn't seen anything on my father's shelves in the last few days that had looked particularly grabbing. I thanked her. "I'll start it tonight," I said.

The feeling of being a youth living in his parents' basement and the excitement of my evening meetups with Kelsey brought with them another familiar feeling: the old, easy, sense of inevitability I'd enjoyed as a teenager. I'd had a sense then that there were tracks laid out before me, and that if I only followed them—stayed on the train, so to speak, and didn't lean too far out to either side—that my life would be an easy one of prosperity and comfort. I hadn't been derailed from these tracks in my last two years of college so much as I'd moved a switch and willfully thrown myself off of them—perhaps because I'd thought doing so would be brave and romantic. However unlikely, the alternative tracks I'd wound up on had now swung back into parallel with my old, original rails. I saw that, by the actions of an immense, golden crane, I might be lifted up and returned to my old, destined way.

We ordered food and watched college bowl games and spy movies in the days that followed, and there was no shortage of holiday toffee, peanut brittle, Topsy's popcorn, or Godiva chocolate. As Kelsey was reluctant to pass time at my father's since he was now home, she and I spent our evenings at the Brush Bar and finished our nights parking at the end of an old access road.

I finished my applications on the afternoon of the thirtieth and drove down River Road, across the bridge, and over the train tracks into town on the morning of the 31st to drop their manilla envelopes off at the Post Office. Afterward I stopped at the Douglas Building and ascended the building's back stairs with a foretaste of the nostalgia I would one day feel for this place I had lived when—think of it!—by a series of missteps and accidents, I had passed four years in the prime of my young adulthood being a humble high school English teacher.

The inside of my apartment was dim, the air stale. The ceilings seemed lower, the doorways and windows more narrow, and the whole of my living room, bedroom, and office smaller and more confining than I remembered them being. I had left a bowl of fruit out on my counter—a handful of apples, two oranges, and a banana—more than a week ago, and they were sunken-in and moldering. Almost bohemian, the way I had lived. It would be a good story to tell.

I watered my dry plants, dumped the fruit into an old grocery bag to take down to the dumpster when I left, and gathered my best dress shirt, my suit in its bag, and a pair of shoes. My father and Sharon had invited me to join them at the country club that night, and some texting with Kelsey had confirmed that she would be attending the club's annual festivities with her parents, too. So I would be ringing in the New Year at the club.

I found a note from my father on the counter when I returned to his place. It said that he and Sharon had gone to do some cleaning at her house, and that they hadn't booked dinner reservations for me when they had made their arrangements, so I would be on my own to eat. Further, though they had tried to get me a space for the festivities after dinner, the table they would be at was already full. My seat for the evening would be at table nineteen. I was free to show up any time after eight-thirty.

I took the first portion of this note to mean that my father and Sharon were planning to move in together soon. In conjunction with the second portion, I understood that I would be on my own at my father's for the next several hours—a prospect I looked forward to with some relish. I couldn't remember a time I had ever been seated anywhere but at one of the first five tables at a club event, so the last part of the note gave me a new prospect to mull over, but I didn't mull it for long. Out the window the herd was out. I picked up the binoculars on the sill and raised them to look at the buffalo grazing on the preserve.

My applications submitted, I didn't have much to do besides padding around the house, visiting the fridge, and watching bowl games that afternoon. At four o'clock, I cracked open the campus novel Sharon had given me for Christmas. At five, I ironed my shirt and shined my shoes, steaming my pants and jacket on the rack in my father's room with his personal steamer. I grilled one on the last steaks from the box in the fridge as the last sunset of the year settled, and poured myself a generous glass of his port to compliment my dinner. My father's Lexus was in the garage—he and Sharon must have taken her jeep to her place—so when the time came to head to the party, I availed myself of the spare key and drove to the clubhouse in style, enjoying the comfort of his heated leather seats.

The clubhouse entrance was festooned with gold and silver streamers, and chintzy metallic boxes, globes, and cones were piled decoratively in the space where the club's eighteen-foot Christmas tree had been a few days before. As I began climbing the stairs toward the Wyatt Earp Banquet Hall, I interpreted this geometric display which I'd never seen before to be a particularly good omen. There was a symbolic importance to celebrating the turn of the New Year at the club with my father, Sharon and Kelsey instead of at the High Plains Oasis or Kemper's with Garret. In my mind's eye, I saw the golden crane beginning to pivot—

But at the top of the stairs, I encountered the same garlanded wreath, the same dangling mistletoe, and the same slow-spinning disco ball I had seen decorating the clubhouse at this time every year since the single-digit years of my youth. It was the same waitstaff wearing the same waitstaff uniforms, the same tables in the same tablecloths with the same settings. The same prime rib carving station. The same buffet. Across the room, my father and Sharon were seated in the same place I was used to seeing my father and mother, and at the table adjacent, Judge Pomerantz and his daughter with her back to me in three-quarters profile. Rather than make my way across the hall to say hello, I paused at the dessert cart nearest the entryway to pick up a slice of key lime pie and ask one of the circulating waitresses to bring me a drink.

Table nineteen was, as I had suspected it would be, the very last of the tables to be filled in the room: slush space for out-of-town aunts and uncles, the newly divorced, and low-status club applicants who were thinking about becoming dues-paying members. The seat with my name card in front of it was the second-to-last open one remaining. A glance at the place card to its right revealed that Jim Morris, Jr had been placed beside me. I recoiled inwardly at the sight of his name, but further inspection revealed that the seat's napkin and silverware were undisturbed and that the sweating water glass had soaked an inch-wide ring into the table-cloth. The country club wasn't Jim Jr's scene, of course. The seat had probably been reserved by his mother, or one of the secretaries at Morris, Able, & Morris. The staff here at the club, knowing him to be a habitual no-show, had relegated his empty seat to the last table. Jim Jr was almost certainly already bellied-up to the front bar at the Oasis, or tipping his chin up toward one of the screens showing the evening's bowl game at Kemper's.

I shook out my napkin and greeted my tablemates, learning that I was, indeed, in the presence of new and applying members and relatives from out-of-town. "Real gem of a golf course," said one of the brother-in-laws upon learning that my father lived at the club. "We come out for your Pro-Am every August. Highlight of my *year*."

I nodded politely, agreed verbally when it became clear such was necessary, and tried not to finish my drink too quickly. Still, it couldn't have been more than a few minutes before the waitress came around, and when she asked for it, I handed her my empty in exchange for a fresh glass.

By sitting up straighter and leaning a little to my right, I found I had a partial view of Kelsey, who was now standing between her father and mother at the front of the room shaking hands with various club members as they came up to offer their New Year's well-wishes. She wore a dress so alike the one her mother was wearing that I wondered if it might *be* her mother's, and generally looked less collegiate and more "country club"—or even "club wife"—than she had at any other time I'd seen her during the break.

It occurred to me then that, despite her soon-to-be-earned JD, "club wife" might be her destined role in life, and "club husband" mine. We might continue to see one another after this romantic holiday break we had shared. She would get her law degree, I'd get mine, and we could both end up practicing in Plains City. We could get married, have kids. She might decide to stop practicing law—or not—and whether or not we decided to live at the club, we would almost certainly be members. Our own children would take tennis, golf, and swim lessons on the club grounds as each of us had. They would be framed between us on nights like this, shaking hands with fellow club members as they came up to pay the respects our family connections and roles in the community warranted, and even if—

The chair beside me jumped backward. A chandelier, or chunk of the ceiling panel, perhaps, had fallen to land on my shoulder. In front of me, all of the table shook. When I turned my head to see if my shirt was torn—to see if I might be bleeding—I saw a baseball-mitt-sized hand. Jim Jr was putting his weight on me as he lowered himself into his seat. "Good to see you, Able. When I heard you were gonna be here, I called Raul and had 'im move me to your table." He picked up his glass and drank it off, then held up his hand to snap his finger and call for a drink. His napkin came up to his lips—he belched—and he turned his eyes to our table-mates. "Howdy," he said. "Jim Morris. Jim Jr, that is. Go by Jim, Jimmy, Jimbo or Junior, take your pick."

Dutifully, I made introductions. Jim shook three men's hands and smiled at their three wives. A waitress brought his new drink and he finished it before setting the glass down on the table. As soon as the conversation shifted away from us he turned to regard me more fully. "So I hear you're joining us in the fold."

"Am I?"

He leaned in. "That's the rumor. And I have to tell you, I think it's a good idea."

"Why's that?"

His hands, which he had folded, broke apart as he lifted them from the table. He held his left wrist up to display the black-faced watch encircling it, tilting it with his right hand so its casing caught the light. "I make a lot of money, bro. A *lot.*"

I nodded, as if this was something I hadn't known or considered. "You aren't concerned I'd be cutting into your profits?"

He leaned back and shook his head. "We've got more than enough business. More than your dad and me can handle, for sure, with my dad retirin'. We're already turning people away and leaving money on the table, tell the truth. If your dad is going to pay for it, I don't know why you wouldn't just hustle off to Lawrence for your two years and get back here to help us scoop it up."

This avenue of conversation suggested an alternative reason for my father's inviting me to the club for New Years. A recruitment dinner: Jim Jr trying to sell me on the law firm. Which, if true, would be ironic. Because Jim Jr, himself, was one of the primary reasons my opinion of the legal profession had fallen off so precipitously near the end of my college career.

As my father's son, I had been raised to hold a high regard for the law, a vocation which so many of the adults in my life—neighbors, teachers, members of the country club, etc.—spoke of with so much reverence. I seldom heard another career, save perhaps "doctor" or "surgeon," referred

to with the same degree of esteem. The word "legal," associated with our formidable stone courthouse, the imposing
mahogany desk in my father's office, and his dark charcoal
and navy suits, had been etched in gold in my mind, where
"medicine,"—scrubs, exam rooms, and replica skeletons
hanging on aluminum posts—was merely silver. A few of
my immediate peers' fathers were doctors; fewer still were
lawyers. And the doctors, when I saw them, always looked
harried and tired. The lawyers took measured steps, seemed
alert and calculating. Beyond these superficial observations
were my understandings of the club and its social pecking
order: the doctors were my father's clients, and he, blessed
with good health, rarely saw his primary care provider for so
much as a checkup. Jim Morris, Jr, two years my senior and
one of my earliest playmates growing up, was the first other
son or daughter of a lawyer I had met, and that he was
stupid—unintelligent, lazy, and dishonest; a rich kid and a
poor student; a known bully in the 6-8 middle school we
both attended, survivor of a drunken jeep rollover in high
school—on the same River Road turn Bryce Davis had
perished on, as it happened—these things had surprised
me. An unfortunate son for such a great man as Jim Sr to
have been saddled with. When I heard during my junior
year of high school that he was embarking on a pre-law
track and planning to apply to law school, my response had
been to feel sorry for him. To think: that Jim Jr thought *he*
could be a lawyer! Lulled into a false sense of capability
because... Why? Because his mother had praised him?
Because his family had money? I was astonished when I
reached the University of Kansas and found he was still an
active student in good standing there. My own mother
somewhat lessened my concern when she told me Jim's
parents were paying for tutoring and that his GPA, as she

understood it, hovered just above the low-water mark for dismissing students from the school. And then he graduated and, to my utter astonishment, was accepted by the law school. Had he even taken the LSAT? My father refused to answer.

I could have easily stopped Jim Jr's line of questioning and told him that I had, in fact, just mailed my applications earlier in the day, but I hadn't even told my father about the applications, yet. I was holding the fact close to my chest, a cherished secret. I sensed I wouldn't like the taste of the words leaving my mouth if I told Jim first.

"It's crossed my mind," I said instead. "But I'm still thinking about it." I looked out across the dining room and caught Kelsey's eye, earning a grin and pair of rolled eyes for finding her.

Jim Jr followed my gaze. "That Judge Pomerantz's daughter?"

I didn't see any harm in being straight with him about her. "We've spent some time together over the break."

Jim grunted his approval. "I wouldn't mind squeezing in there. But isn't she seeing somebody?"

I turned back to see if he was messing with me. "Is she?"

He reached his right hand across to his left shoulder and tapped it three times, as if this gesture helped him recall things, or indicated a brand of 'scout's honor.' "Some big shot, I think. In Kansas City."

"*Big shot*, how?"

"Lawyer. Big firm up there. *Big*."

I asked him where he had heard this, and when.

"My mom. 'Bout a month ago? Maybe six weeks?"

I looked back across the room. Kelsey was involved in a conversation with her father and Dean Atchley, the city planner. "I might ask her."

"Yeah," he advised as I rose and began to push my chair back in. "I dunno if I'd do that."

She saw me coming and met me midway through the ballroom. "How are the cheap seats?" she asked, her eyes laughing. I looked back. Even from the middle of the room, table nineteen looked like a far-off outpost, the stuffed and mounted heads of several hunted animals foreign and menacing on the wall behind it.

"Not so bad where the deer and the buffalo roam. Want to dance?" I began to move toward the dance floor, but she didn't move with me. I turned.

"I don't dance at these things."

"Because as a UN delegate, it's beneath your dignity?"

She tilted her head. "Why UN delegate?"

I motioned up and down to reference her dress.

"When I'm out with my parents—"

"Forget it." I understood what it meant to be out with one's parents. "I turned in my applications," I said in order change the subject to something more positive, but the stare she returned was a blank one. "For my law schools and those graduate programs. I dropped them in the mail this morning."

The look *this* intelligence elicited wasn't one I had anticipated. "You're not applying to—"

"Law school," I said again. "And a few graduate programs."

"Aren't you happy here teaching social studies and coaching basketball?"

"I don't teach social studies. I teach *English*. And I don't coach."

"But you were such a good player," she began, then switched tacks. "You're not doing this for me, are you?" The look on her face now wasn't quite horrified, but it was close. I took a half-step back.

"No, I was always applying. Didn't we talk—"

"Schools, like many?"

"Not just the one you're at," I clarified. "And not for you. I really didn't tell you I was filling out applications?"

She shook her head. Ransacking my memory to check my mental tape, I suddenly saw how this could have been the case. The two of us hadn't done a lot of talking.

"I'm not sure that I could—I mean, I'm pretty busy with my studies, and I'm not really interested in—" she stammered.

"Are you seeing someone else? Jim Jr said he thought you were seeing someone in Kansas City."

She reddened. There was no laughter in her eyes, now. "He and I—it's weird."

"And you and I?"

"A vacation thing?"

I nodded. "He's got a job in Kansas City, and you're a serious student. You and I are... a vacation thing."

A new song came on and she glanced over to the dance floor. "Do you want to—"

I shook my head.

"Maybe we could—"

"No. I think I ought to head out."

Her bottom lip came out. "We could still—"

"It was fun," I offered.

"It was," she agreed.

Jim Jr watched me approach. For all the dullness I had always attributed him, he sized the situation up pretty quickly. "Better to've loved and lost," he said. "And you got your rocks off, right?"

"I think I'm going to head out."

"Stick around." He held up a new glass. "Drinks are paid for. We can go down to the Brush Bar later and see the young people."

I shook my head.

"You sure? We could pick up some biddies and head back to my place. I've got a hot tub under some propane lamps. I've been looking for an excuse to fire 'em up."

"No," I said. The words *vacation thing* echoed in my ears. My own vacation, I felt, was over. "I need to get home and sleep in my own bed. I want to start the new year in my own place."

Jim Jr's look became morose. "Seems stupid to let her ruin your night." I watched as, like a sullen child, he scraped the edge of his fork around the perimeter of his pie plate.

"The hot tub sounds good. We'll do it another time." I lifted my jacket from the back of my chair.

When the fireworks began exploding an hour later I was in my father's basement, packing the last of my things, and I saw the dying glow of a high school party over the top of a rise I knew as I navigated River Road. I could imagine Javi and Marcos and a dozen of my other first block students circling a bonfire as I and my classmates had done almost a decade before. On the fourth floor of the Douglas building, a cloud of smoke thick enough to obscure the door of my apartment met me when the elevator doors opened; I feared the building was on fire, wondered if someone had already called the fire department or if I would have to. But then I heard laughter and smelled cigarettes and burned bacon. It wasn't a fire, but a not-unroutine post-midnight cooking mishap. At the end of the hall I made out a number of young people—both college and high school students— pointing and doubled over in laughter. I saw Adrienne from my first-block class, I thought, but couldn't quite tell.

Whoever it was disappeared through an open door too quickly.

I took a towel from my closet and shoved it into the gap between my floor and the bottom of my door to keep the smoke out, then began flipping on light switches and turning on lamps. In contrast to how small it had seemed when I'd swung by earlier, my apartment now seemed decently-sized and cozy: my rooms with my things, decorated the way I had done the place up. In particular, I was glad to see my jacketless Merriam Webster Collegiate Dictionary, clothbound in red, which I might now have a few days of carefully balanced meals on while I sat on my couch watching television.

That Kelsey Pomerantz had misjudged me and used me in the last week—that she had thought I was a social studies teacher, a basketball coach, *a vacation thing*—didn't bother me so much now that I was home. I could see that she couldn't have known *me*, that I hadn't accurately or honestly represented myself to her. That she, too, had been a 'vacation thing.' And that this could be fine: something I might smile about later. Likely someday soon. In the meantime, it was a new year and closing in on time for me to go to bed. Time to start reading a new play. Something weighty: one I had been putting off for a while, working to get into proper 'reading shape' for before plucking it down off my shelf. "Happy New Year, Billy," I said, and finger-tipped my old, university bookstore-stickered copy of *Hamlet* down from its place. I thought I would read just a scene or two, until Hamlet and the ghost had their conversation, but that exchange turned out to be in the fifth scene, not one of the first two or three, so I stayed up until after two and slept in past ten before waking up in my own bed on the first day of the new year.

PART II

On Tuesday morning the books were gone.

I didn't see it at first. At first it only seemed that the lines of the student desks in my room stood out more sharply against the floor than they had two weeks before—as if the room now, in January, somehow admitted of more light than it had in December. I wondered if the janitors had waxed the floors, or washed the windows. Or if maybe some of the furniture was missing: a table or bookshelf. But no, as far as I could tell, all of the furniture was where it belonged.

I looked to the nearest student desks, which still had pencil markings and eraser curls on them from the first-semester final. Then I squatted down to look at the floor, found it still scuffed and covered in dust. The windows appeared unwashed, and the anodized aluminum legs and metal baskets slung beneath the desks unpolished. –And then I saw it, or began to register what I didn't see. Leaning forward to balance my weight on two fingers, I pivoted right, then left, and saw that the metal baskets that had formerly cradled my junior- and senior-level textbooks were empty.

This, in itself, didn't mean much. The janitors might have moved the desks for some reason. They might have removed the books from the baskets to facilitate this process. When I craned my neck toward the back counters to see if the books had been stacked there, I saw that *they* were empty—that the dictionaries and thesauruses and student vocabulary workbooks that I had formerly stacked there were gone.

I crossed the room, opened my cabinets. Gone were my squirreled-away copies of *Gatsby*, *Inherit the Wind*, and *Fences*. Gone were *The Awakening*, *A Raisin in the Sun*, and *Of Mice and Men*. Gone my Norton volumes of poetry, my Bedford Editions of short fiction from which I had planned to teach my upcoming unit on short stories by American women.

I stepped back and sat on the nearest of the unwashed desks. They had cleaned me out. Tired of my hijinks and evasions, the Head of Literacy had deployed the janitorial staff to come in and box up my materials. Begrudgingly, I almost respected her for it. Not that I wouldn't find a way to work around it—I still had paper copies of the short stories that I planned to start the semester with; I would still find my way into the book closet and get my hands on the novels I wanted my students to read. I would just have to store the books more carefully. I might check them out to the students and have them keep them at home. We could devote our class time to bookless discussions, or I could make copies of particular pages and practice close reading and annotation strategies...

After a time, I rose and went to my desk. Opening my email, I found a long chain of exchanged messages—much longer than I would have expected for the first workday back to school. The book removal—the *heist*, as Mrs.

Dennison called it—hadn't been limited to my classroom. *All* of the English teachers' rooms had been ransacked over the break. *All* of the books in the English classrooms had been taken. *No one* had escaped the administrators' notice. I traced the chain of messages back to its origin. Mrs. Rosenbaum had come into the building to do some work on the twenty-fourth. The books were already gone then.

An icon on my screen blinked and I clicked it. There was a meeting, it said, scheduled for all of the teachers in the department. It was taking place in Mrs. Rosenbaum's room. It had begun five minutes ago.

When I arrived, the first thing that surprised me was how crowded the room was. It wasn't just the English teachers, Mr. Russel, Mr. Avery, and Mrs. Hirsche, as I had expected. All six of the school's principals were present. In addition, Mr. Backus, the district's Head of Instruction, was leaning back against the rear wall in his ill-fitting suit, and Bob Cress, the district's silver-haired Superintendent, was seated at Mrs. Rosenbaum's desk, his gold pen aloft. I slipped into a student seat and slid my hands over the cool surface of its attached surface.

The second thing to surprise me as I acclimated to the room was that it wasn't Mrs. Dennison or one of the other English teachers whose ranting I had heard from outside in the hall, but that of Mrs. Hirsche. She was standing at Mrs. Rosenbaum's podium, her face contorted in anger.

"*We* didn't want to take them. *You* made us. Your department had *years* to raise the test scores, and you didn't raise them. You had *years* to work with the district on a meaningful plan of action, and you refused to work with us. *We* in the district office..."

She sounded not so much like a reading specialist charged with improving test scores as an abusive partner explaining her assault to her victim. I looked for another member of my department with whom to share this thought, but all of my fellow teachers were in front of me facing forward, taking the scolding as impassively as so many uncontrite students had taken so many scoldings before.

When Mrs. Hirsche at last finished, Mrs. Rosenbaum raised her hand. "But we *have* raised the scores, Janine. We've raised them by more than twenty-five points since the first year the test was administered." This was true. We *had* raised our scores. We just hadn't raised them quickly enough to hit the moving target of the federal expectations.

"And we *did* participate and offer suggestions for the plan of action," Mrs. Dennison added, her voice more plaintive and beseeching than I'd heard it before. "We spent *months* creating test prep plans and materials. *Summer* months."

Mrs. Hirsche purpled.

"If I may," said Bob Cress, rising from his seat to stand near the front of the room. "All that Janine wants—all that *any* of us wants—is for the kids to pass the dag-mum tests. We in the district office have felt our sense of urgency is... greater than yours here in your classrooms. That you're still dallying in outmoded modes of education instead of actively engaging with us in new-school ways." Mr. Cress waved away the raised hands this comment elicited. "We have, what, eight weeks until the tests this year? And we're going to pass the things. And then we're going to get to work passing next year's tests, and then the tests the year after that. For three years. Because we are professional educators, because this is what's required of us, and because we *can*. If any of you is no longer a professional educator—or feels you are not up to the challenge of being a professional educator—we in the district office will accept your letter of resignation. Now what me and Mrs. Hirsche and Mr. Backus here believe..."

I looked off to my right where the once-crowded bookshelves beneath the windows now stood desolate, their middles sagging under weight that was no longer there. The room had been Mrs. Unger's when I was a student; a few desks away was the seat I had occupied when I had read *The Odyssey*, *A Midsummer Night's Dream*, and *The Adventures of Huckleberry Finn*. Scanning the emptied shelves, I could still remember where several of Mrs. Unger's class sets of books had stood—*The Scarlet Letter, The Women of Brewster Place, A Farewell to Arms*. Here was where *Fahrenheit-451* had been, and there *Catch-22*. The mere existence of these last two books should have precluded a meeting like this from ever taking place. But then, Bob Cress, Janine Hirsche and Chad Backus weren't the kinds of people who would likely have read and appreciated Bradbury or Heller.

When I was a freshman studying *The Odyssey* in Mrs. Unger's room, we had been assigned groups, and in these groups had used cardstock to create frames within which to arrange cut-up and torn pieces of tissue paper, red and blue, yellow and green, orange and purple, gluing one piece to another using orange Elmer's glue sticks to present scenes from Homer's epic: The Sirens, The Underworld, The Swine: "stained glass windows" that we taped to the actual windows, bathing the room in a soft, gauzy pink light. What standards and benchmarks might Mrs. Hirsche have ticked off on her clipboard had she walked into that class? *Students Work in Collaborative Teams*? *Students Appreciate Mythological Contexts*? I doubted Mrs. Hirsche or any of our administrators would have smiled on Mrs. Unger's use of class time that day, but to me, now, it seemed that we had *Made Art*, and, perhaps even more importantly, *Made Friends.* Because Elizabeth Selvage and Harmony Arteaga and Chase Cleary and I hadn't *been* friends before we had worked together on that in-class project, but we had been friends afterward. We had, over the next four years, nodded to one another in hallways, shared tables at lunch, and piled into cars with one another after school.

"—*teach the assigned curriculum*," Mrs. Hirsche said with some vehemence, and the meeting ended. We were released. Mrs. Rosenbaum, Mrs. Dennison, and Valerie Stephens rose to ply their cases in hushed voices more privately, and the rest of us atomized dazedly into the halls.

IF I WAS ANGRY—OUTRAGED—INCREDULOUS—THEN these emotions were muted partially by the fact that I had already spent so much time in the last twenty months being angry, outraged, and incredulous. They were also partially muted by the fact I didn't have *time* to engage with them. Deprived of the books I had planned to make use of the next day, I needed to scramble to prepare other materials. I spent the rest of the morning planning, and passed the afternoon sifting through the piles of district materials I had been given over the last three semesters to find the worksheets and packets that seemed least bad, then went home feeling, not freshened at the conclusion of my winter's break, but depleted by the revelations of the day.

"Mis-tah *Able!*" Javi sang out as he bounced into my classroom the next morning. "You are *not* gonna believe what this fool Marcos did over the break. First, he *falls in love.* Then he *loses his shoes.* Brand new pair of Adaidays—" He paused, looked me over. "You good, Mr. A?"

"I'm good," I told him. "Just getting back into the swing."

He nodded and was off to the races—telling me how Marcos had gotten up the nerve to ask out Marie Peron, a senior forward on the girls soccer team, and how she had consented to go out with him; how Marcos was 'whipped' now, and didn't have any time for his boys. How the beautiful, immaculately-white pair of Adidas had been set on top of a car while Marcos was talking to Marie, forgotten, and then lost forever when said car drove off... "What about you? You have a good break?" he wanted to know, and then the bell rang, and the new semester, too, was off to the races.

"Alright, okay, let's settle," I said, standing in the front center of the room and moving my hands in ways my students were familiar with. "It's good to see you all; I hope you had good breaks." I guided them first through a reflective write over the first semester, then a goal-setting exercise for this second one. Then I lifted a stack of multiple-choice bubblers from the inside shelf of my podium.

"We doing these again?" Marcos asked when he saw them.

"It's good to work on skills," I said, trying to speak lightly. "You guys do drills in football and basketball practice, right?"

Warily, several of their heads nodded.

"That's all we're doing, trying to work on fundamentals."

Trained from their earliest youths to obey the dictates of their coaches, half my class nodded and reached for their pencils. "There won't be any outside homework as long as we're doing these practices," I added. This seemed to do the trick for the rest of them: my students became pliant and bent to their task.

I found that the anger I hadn't had time to possess in the first few days of the semester gradually rose in me in the days that followed. Part of this had to do with how pliant my students were. They *trusted* me, and thought I was delivering them an appropriate education—an education roughly equivalent to the educations their peers in Wichita and Kansas City and on the far-off coasts of our country were getting. One that would give them the contexts they needed to understand the world around them and initiate them as members of our culture, set them up for college, prepare them for the workplace. Get them ready for *life*. And here I was, in reality, preparing them for a test whose passage would be far more helpful to the Head of Literacy and the Superintendent's careers than any of their own.

I began to have a problem roughly opposite to the one I'd had a few months before. Not the divided sleep I had experienced born of despair, but a near-inability to sleep on account of my now constant, low-simmering fury. As if a faulty adrenal gland had become stuck in the 'On' position, pouring high-octane fuel into my bloodstream and kicking my heart into a permanent state of high rev, so I had to seek out exhaustion by taking long walks and going to the gym after school. Even hard four and five o'clock workouts proved temporary palliatives at best. If I was exhausted at six or seven, I still had to go on other, farther walks after dinner, at ten o'clock, at midnight. The sleep I did find was brief; when I woke at two, three, or four o'clock in the morning my heart raced again, reminding me of my pre-game nerves before important high school basketball games, only now the anxiety never lifted because the game never began.

On a particular Thursday, perhaps the fourth or fifth of the semester, Mrs. Hirsche walked into my room while my students were working on their packets. We had already cleared two practice pages and were working through a third. I was walking the classroom's perimeter, proctoring, and had 'start' and 'stop' times written on the board. My students in Jock English, well-coached, were engrossed in their efforts. I saw a hint of pleasure on the Head of Literacy's face as she began to mark down her 'demographic' and 'survey' notes for the room.

"That's time," I said, though there were still four more minutes remaining in this round of the practice. "Put your pencils down."

Marcos pointed toward the front board. "Uh, Mr. Able—"

"Turn over your packets," I said.

"Ain't gotta tell me twice," said Javi. He slapped down his yellow #2 and flipped over his packet.

"We're done for the day. You guys can get your phones out, or talk amongst yourselves." I walked over to my desk and sat down, opened my email. In the back of the room, Mrs. Hirsche stayed until her ten minutes were up, then walked out. My only real regret was that she might have marked off a box or two based on what she'd seen when she first walked in. If I could have arranged it so that she'd walk out with an unchecked-form, I would have.

16

L auren West came to visit me during the first week of February, the only time during the school year she stepped into my classroom. The school day had let out fifteen minutes before, and I was tipped back in my chair, a leg over the corner of my desk, paging through *Great Expectations* in search of suitable passages to pull out for test-prep. Thinking her a student, I held up a finger. "Just let me finish this paragraph."

She didn't say anything, and when I looked up, the sight of her so startled me as to make me drop the front legs of my chair to the floor. A lot of people had had a rough school year—Mrs. Rosenbaum had come down with the flu after Thanksgiving and needed to miss ten days, and Ms. Kominski, from math, had recently had to be admitted to the hospital for pneumonia. I had recently experienced a resurgence of the molar grinding that had plagued me during first semester, and had resumed my nightly use of Dr. Hill's appliance. But Ms. Kominski had only looked a little thinner the last time I had seen her, and Mrs. Rosenbaum looked about the same now as she always had. Lauren West looked worn and emaciated, as if the school year that had advanced the rest of us six months in our lives thus far had added five years of hard living to her own. Her shoulders were hunched up as if in permanent expectation of being surprised, and there were dark serifs below her eyes.

"Where did you get these?" she asked. "I don't have these."

She was at my podium, leafing through my handouts. "I made them," I told her.

She looked up and frowned. "We're allowed to make our own?"

"No. But I couldn't keep using the ones they're giving us. They're awful."

She picked up the top one, looked at it more closely. "This is good. You make these on your plan?"

"At night, before I go to bed. They actually don't take that long. An hour or so usually. Sometimes just forty-five minutes."

She looked back down at the handout, flipped it over. "You're using passages from the banned books?"

"The banned books and some books they haven't banned yet."

"And you don't get written up?"

"No one ever looks. As long as they see stapled packets of paper, the admins are mostly happy."

She set the handout down, turned to look at the writing on my marker board.

"Did you need help with something?"

When she sat down on one of the desks in my front row, it was with more weight than I'd have credited her for carrying. She looked to the ceiling as if for strength and took a breath. "I hear you're a person who can get students to pass the test."

"Not all of them."

"Anything you could tell me would be helpful. They have us in these new teachers meetings. With Mr. Avery and Mrs. Hirsche? They're twice a week after school, but they keep saying the same things over and over and I'm not sure either of them knows anything about what they're talking about."

I felt myself grimace. "Do you know about the test? What's on it?"

She threw up her hands. "Standards. The test is on the standards."

"But they've told you about the format, right?"

"It's three days. It has short passages. It's multiple-choice."

So she didn't really know. Standing, I picked up a dry erase marker from my board's tray. "I'm going to lecture at you. Are you okay with being lectured?"

She shrugged. "I can be okay."

"Start at the start, there are a hundred and twenty-five questions." I wrote *125* on the board. "Six or seven passages, depending, and one or two sets of short questions that aren't associated with any passages. Three days to take the whole thing. Two or three of the passages are narrative, two or three argumentative, two informational. Call it two passages one day, two the other, and three on the third. Both of the two-passage days get a small battery of miscellaneous questions apart from the passages. So forty questions on two days and forty-five the other, designed to take an on-level kid about sixty or seventy-five minutes. A really bright kid can get through in thirty-five or forty; a kid who works slower but can do it might take an hour and a half or two hours, depending. If a kid wants to stay after the testing block ends, you let them. The number one piece of advice you give your students is that there's no time limit, so they ought to take as long as they need. If you can remove the stigma of taking a long time, you'll go a long way toward getting your kids to pass."

Ms. West nodded. "Okay."

"They don't want to do it, of course. Most of them don't have the attention span, or the patience, or the motivation to care. I tell them they can take a bathroom break or get a drink if they want—it's allowed—and I encourage them to use it if I think they're getting sleepy. You should buy some bags of peppermints and hard candies for them to suck on, and some packs of cinnamon and spearmint chewing gum. Let them have as much as they want—the smells and little bits of sugar keep them awake.

"The length of the test is the biggest hurdle. Almost no one in the school gives hour-long exams anymore, and your lowest-achieving kids aren't in shape for an hour and a half-long test, much less three tests back-to-back-to-back. No matter what you do, your attendance rates are going to drop off after the first day, and you're going to have to track kids down to come in during the make-up times. When they ditch, you can't get mad at them. You have to keep it upbeat and positive and make sure they know you're on their side. Tell them the scores are used for course placement, and remind them about the remediation classes for kids who fail. Tell them they don't want to be in them if they can help it. The scores aren't used for college or scholarships right now, but you can tell them that might change. It's definitely part of their permanent records. Whatever you do, don't tell them to do it for the school or as a favor to you."

She shook her head. "I wouldn't think of it."

"If anything, tell them to have some pride and do it for themselves. On the last day you'll have a few who've done the work the first two days and want to give up early. You've got to address that in advance. I mean, don't belabor the point or turn them off with it, but address it. Before you go to the testing rooms on the last day, remind them how hard they've worked. Encourage them to, you know, see it through. Do you have any questions?"

As if a weary, sullen student herself, she had begun to stare at the floor during the last part of my speech. She looked up now. "Is it hard?"

"The test?" I could have laughed. "The test is easy. It's on, like, an eighth-grade level mostly, with two or three sections that're harder. Like sophomore or junior hard. The hard part is the length—the wear-down factor."

"So—"

"So it's a three-day marathon and we've got kids who wouldn't finish strong if it was a sprint, who don't see the point of sitting through four and a half hours-worth of assessments that don't count toward their grades. The administrators come in during inservices and tell us to build lessons in twenty-minute increments to accommodate our students' supposed twenty-minute attention spans, and now we have kids who can't even do things for twenty minutes."

"The test is easy," she repeated. There was a look of bewilderment on her face.

"Easier every year."

"Why?"

"The Fed requires us to clear a higher pass rate every year, and they let the states make their own tests. What would you do?"

She mulled this over. "How much easier?"

"A few less of the hardest questions, and the hardest passages get either a little shorter or a little more straight forward. The vocabulary gets a little more accessible. The context clues become more pointed."

"Because they have to hit a hundred percent passage in the next five years."

"Because it's an impossible task. Because it's economically advantageous to make it look like we have a better educational system than Oklahoma or Missouri or Colorado or Nebraska."

Lauren blinked. "And nobody checks up on this sort of thing?"

"People know. Lots of people. But it's like anything else. 'Wisdom cries out in the streets' and all that."

As if she was one of my students, I counted off the seconds of wait time while she processed this. "Are you sure?"

"The tests the kids took in the first two or three years were closer to being like college entrance exams. There were excerpts from hundred-year-old newspaper editorials and passages translated from the Greek or Latin. Vocabulary words like 'recondite' and 'esoteric.' The narrative questions required students to comprehend abstract symbols, make difficult inferences, and draw abstract conclusions. There were 'most likely means' questions where kids had to work in gray areas. The new tests are made up of passages from magazines like *Field and Stream* and *Time*. The vocab is easier. More questions are more objective. On the original tests, less than half of the questions were the kind where you could put your finger on part of the passage and find your answer. The new tests are seventy or eighty percent like that."

"So it isn't so much a reading test as a 'let's see how willing the kids are to do the work' test."

"They can't all pass, but most of them can. If they try.

Beyond seeing if they *can* read, it's hardly even a test of how well they read. It's really a test of how much they care—of how much we've convinced them to care."

A NEW QUOTE appeared on the wall of the English department office later that week. John Milton, from Areopagitica: "As good almost kill a man as kill a good book: Who kills a man kills a reasonable creature, God's image; but he who destroys a good book kills reason itself." There were Christmas lights around it, the old lights we used to string up during the English Department's annual white elephant gift exchanges.

As good almost kill a man as kill a good book. There were parts of books scattered all over my desk at home—excerpts from Charles Dickens, Nathaniel Hawthorne, Charlotte Bronte, and Mary Shelley—excerpts I had copied by flattening their parent books on the glass of the school and public library's Xerox machines. Excerpts I had literally cut apart with scissors and pasted back together with glue. Was I killing books? In my classroom, I taught my students to treat the test as if they were preparing for a game. There were so many points possible, so many that must be earned. The rules and parameters of the game were clear; the ways the game might unfold predictable. Since the test was multiple choice, test takers didn't necessarily have to understand a passage or know answers cold; there were strategies they could use to gamble, like the process of elimination, and there were patterns that the tests followed. *This is the kind of question the test makers are likely to ask*, I had said on more than one occasion. *These are the types of 'both/ and' dummy answers they like to include. Answer stems with this type of extra wordiness are almost never the correct answer.* There were ways of gaming the system, and I had taught them every one I knew. When I was finished, what had I accomplished?

He who destroys a good book kills reason itself. That's what I was doing, wasn't it? Cutting books down to excerpts, reducing novels to statements of theme? I'd spent the better part of the last two years hating the administration for removing the literature from my classroom, but wasn't I, by teaching to the test, doing the same thing?

17

I woke at six on the first morning of Spring Break, this by force of habit. I'd have liked to go back to sleep, but try as I might, I couldn't. Instead I rose, dressed, finger-combed my hair, and made my way downstairs to stand in the vestibule between the elevator and the door to Wonder's waiting for the bakery to open, becoming, when it did so, the first person of the day to walk in and order a Danish and cappuccino. I had been sitting for perhaps twenty-five minutes, leafing through a day-old copy of the *Post-Dispatch*, when Lauren West walked in, her white puffer jacket, brisk step, and the sunglasses on her head suggesting a road trip in her immediate future.

She paced over to my table after placing her order. "You were right," she said, taking her gloves off.

"Right about?"

"About this being a terrible place to work. You know, 'where educational dreams go to die.'"

"Did I say that?"

"It's what you told me at the Oasis. That night after your

student's... passing. I thought—well, I just thought you were being an asshole."

"I've got that in me."

"But you weren't wrong. It's not a good place to teach—or learn. Did your kids do okay on the test?"

The state tests had taken place on Monday, Tuesday, and Wednesday the previous week, with make-ups on Thursday and Friday. The 'raw' scores populated on the tests' computer screens after the students were finished, so we knew roughly how well we had done. "I passed more than I failed. You?"

"Eighty-six percent," she said. Her smile took on a different quality—she seemed genuinely pleased.

The cutoff for the year was eighty-five. "You cleared."

"And you?"

I shrugged. "Ninety-two or ninety-three? We did okay." The smile on her face remained, but some of the brightness went out of her eyes. It looked as if, in her mind, my accomplishment diminished her own. "Eighty-six is amazing for a first-year, though. I only cleared... I think it was seventy-five my first year."

Her eyes brightened back up. "I heard Rosenbaum did ninety-four, and Stephens hit ninety. We might have passed as a school."

She looked so hopeful that I decided not to bring up the trouble of 'subgroups'—the fact that we had a particularly high number of demographic subcategories—race and gender classifications further divided by socio-economic categories, Special Education status, and English Language Learner classifications. There were usually one or two that we came up short in, and so we would be deemed 'failures' even if the student body on the whole passed the test.

Because of some of her certifications and training, Mrs. Dennison generally taught a number of these harder-to-pass students. I'd heard her pass-rate was somewhere in the neighborhood of seventy-nine. "We might," I said. "We'll know in a month or so, I guess."

The waitress brought Lauren her drink in a paper cup and handed her a folded-over white paper bag already going translucent from the stickiness of whatever was inside.

"Heading out of town?" I asked.

"I'm going back to Illinois. My parents live north of Chicago."

"Sounds good. Travel safe."

"See you after the break." By the way she waved, I wondered if we might be on the path to becoming friends.

I WENT for a walk after my breakfast, and found, to my dismay, that it wasn't even nine-thirty yet when I walked back into to my apartment. The length of the Spring Break week yawned out desolately before me.

My copy of *Hamlet* was resting on my end table where I had left it the night in early January before I'd returned to school; after discovering my books had been taken, I hadn't made any further progress in it. The page I had bookmarked was near the end of the fourth act and featured Horatio reading a letter from Hamlet discussing his abduction by pirates—*pirates?*—which I didn't recall at all. I decided to back up and start the fourth act again.

I finished the play before lunch, went for another walk, and ate a sandwich while watching television in my living room. A north wind whistled against the side of the building. Either because I had read the first half of the play two months before—and thus didn't have a good sense of the whole—or because it just didn't do it for me, I wasn't sure I thought much of what I had been given to understand was Shakespeare's greatest play. Maybe this itself was the problem: that *Hamlet* had been so highly acclaimed that my expectations were impossible to meet. I *liked* the play, to be sure, but I wasn't sure I *loved* it. And when I thought about teaching it in class, I didn't feel any of the special enthusiasm I knew I would need to summon to kindle my students' interest. The betrayal and revenge were fine, as was the ruinous culmination of the play, what with almost all of the principal characters dying, but the adolescent, namesake protagonist dominated almost to the exclusion of the rest of the cast. And more than anything, his hamartia bothered me. What kind of tragic flaw was *hesitancy*? It didn't seem as weighty or significant as greed, pride, lust, ambition, or even naïveté. And while I got some pleasure out of Hamlet's adolescent angst, I wasn't sure my students would. My athletes, I didn't think, would have much patience for his neuroses. "Quit your bitchin'" was almost a catchphrase for them. And so many of the speeches were long, and so much of the action and soliloquizing would need explaining, and, when it was all said and done, I wasn't sure I really *got* the play myself.

I wondered if William Gramley might have anything to say about it in his chapter on the Elizabethan poet's works, so as the wind howled I picked up my copy of *Stories Don't Matter in the Real World* and began to reread its last chapter:

Of the many beliefs I have arrived at over my twenty-seven years in the English and Language Arts classroom, perhaps the

*one I hold with the greatest conviction is this: that the greatest
goal of a high school English curriculum ought to be to teach the
comedies, histories, and tragedies of William Shakespeare.
Despite—or perhaps because of—the fact this view has become
an increasingly unpopular one, under siege by administrators,
school boards, and business-minded lobbying interests alike, I find
that this conviction strengthens with each year which passes and
each group of students I usher through the hallowed experience of
reading a play...*

While Gramley offered a glowing endorsement of the
bard, a number of well-reasoned arguments for Shakespeare's inclusion in modern curricula, and several anec-
dotes about his own teaching of Elizabethan drama, there
wasn't anything specific about teaching *Hamlet* in the chapter. Which was just as well. He had given me an idea: I
would teach a Shakespearean play to my juniors when we
got back from the break. I had already read several I thought
they might like. Before I decided, I thought I would knock
out *Othello*, and so have finished all four of the "great
tragedies" before making my decision.

And *Othello*, as soon as I started it, floored me.

"Tush, never tell me!" Roderigo says to Iago to kick off
the play, and "'SBlood," the other replies. As the first few
pages unfolded, I could see a Venetian street at night among
that city's fabled canals transmuted to a wide Plains City
road lined by single-story houses with heat-browned yards
on a hot summer day.

"Tell me about it!" or "Get the fuck out of here!"
Roderigo was saying, and "I ain't fucking lying!" or "Shut up
and listen, fool," was Iago's response. Except it wasn't
Roderigo and Iago, but Marcos and Javi. As I turned the
pages—Iago pontificating on those honest knaves who serve
their masters as opposed to those soulful fellows who line

their own coats... Roderigo standing in the light to call up to Brabantio while Iago race-baited Desdemona's father from the shadows... Othello arguing for the purity of his love... Desdemona explaining how she fell in love with the Moorish general and both coaxed and coached him to love her—I knew the play was the one I had to teach.

I went out with Garret that night and had dinner with my father the next. That Monday, the third day of my week off from school, I began to doubt the certainty with which I had decided to teach the play. If *Othello* was Shakespeare's great play about race, as I had heard an old college professor term it, wouldn't it be a little 'on the nose' for me to teach it to my students? The last thing my majority-minority students needed was their white teacher using a play by a DWM to teach them about racism. But then on Tuesday I finished reading it, and found that, more than being Shakespeare's great treatment of race, the play was about manipulation and the ways we leave ourselves prey to the ministrations of those who would manipulate us. And everywhere I looked, from the business owners who wanted to hire my students for hard, low-wage work, to the advertisers who dangled the promises of sex and status to sell them body sprays and new cars, to the political pundits on the major network news channels raising their voices with fake rage and indignation, I saw that the world was filled with Iagos who wanted to lead my students astray. Teaching the play would be a way to inoculate my students against these grasping Machiavellis—or at least offer them fair warning.

In my imagined teachings of the play I saw Javi playing Roderigo, Marcos Othello, the baseball team's Danny Ruiz as Cassio, and Adrienne as Desdemona. I saw my students sitting up straighter on the first page when the talk turned to

abhorrence and hate, scratching their heads as Iago
proclaimed "I am not what I am." They would narrow their
eyes at the race-baiting of Brabantio, delight in the opportunity to act out the riot in the second act. I would take particular care in parsing out the third scene of Act III. How was
it, exactly, that Iago lured Othello into jealous madness?
How much should we credit Iago's devious machinations?
How much was it Othello's own fault? And how alike are we
to Othello in our vulnerability to having our hopes and inse-
curities preyed upon? How much outsized impact could a
token as seemingly trivial as a handkerchief have on our
own lives?

Dubious of my ability to get into the school's book room
after the break ended, and unsure whether I would find
copies of the play there if I *could* get in, I found a place
online where I could order slim Dover copies of *Othello* for a
dollar ninety-five apiece and paid an extra twelve dollars for
rush shipping.

I went out with Garret again that Friday night, and
Saturday the weather turned. The wind that had been
coming in from the north shifted to the south, and Sunday
was bright, in the upper seventies, with promises of the
eighties in the week ahead. I opened my windows to let in
some fresh air, as did almost every other tenant in my building, and could hear, reverberating from the brick roads
below and brick walls across the way, the sounds of conversations, music, afternoon movies, and televised sporting
events floating through the air. Around two thirty I caught a
whiff of pot, the odor of which has always struck me as
unpleasant and a little bit sinister. Any other day I might
have risen and shut my windows against it, but on this
particular day, my books having arrived and my plans for
teaching in place, the scent seemed only mildly transgres-

sive, perhaps even festive. Reminiscent of the celebrations in the second act of the play I was about to teach, after the Turkish fleet had been wrecked by a storm and drifted to the bottom of the Mediterranean. An omen, then: a foretaste of my own change of luck in the classroom after the break.

18

B y the Friday of our first week back after Spring Break, my daily attendance rates in free fall, the students I *did* have in the room pushing back hard against me, I couldn't remember why I'd thought teaching *Othello* would go so well to begin with. How could I have thought I could walk into my classroom carrying a box of dense, 400-year-old plays like gifts and expect my students to accept them as such? "Are you for real?" Marcos had wanted to know, and, "Nah, man. I ain't even tryna read that right now," said Javi. Even Adrienne had looked up at me through her parted bangs with skepticism, as if trying to determine whether I was making a joke or not.

The weather was warm, verging on hot—the mercury risen much higher than the weather reports had anticipated—and as they came into my room every day, my students were dressed as if for a field trip to the city pool and basketball courts, not a day of class. The boys wore sleeveless Nike t-shirts and AND1 shorts; the girls had donned dress code-defying halter tops, spaghetti straps, and cut-off shorts. Furtively and with undisguised interest, my students' eyes roved the room as they caught up, settling on one another as if newly exposed arms, legs, clavicles, and cleavage, and not the books I had brought, were the long-suppressed texts we ought to be studying.

I waved my hands to settle them down, and then after I'd shared my plan for the coming weeks had to wave my hands and settle them again. The fact that I wanted them to start reading a play—that I wanted to use their assigned *English* class time to assign them a reading in *English*—appeared to strike a number of them as unjust—a betrayal. *We did your test,* was their not quite fully-articulated sentiment. And: *This is our time.* For me, the image I'd had in my mind of handing out my copies of *Othello* and starting to read the play in class—a triumphant scene I had first loosely sketched, then carefully filled-in brushstroke after brushstroke over the break—had become an old-world masterpiece in my mind, something fit to display in a museum. My students' first dragging their feet over the next few days, and then digging in their heels, was like a splash of bright red paint thrown across it.

Too late, I remembered I needed to establish context, lay groundwork, and build anticipation—that just because *I* was excited didn't mean that they would be. Springing the play on them cold had been a rookie mistake. By the time I had backpedaled and started these necessary activities, I'd lost three-quarters of the class. A bitching-and-moaning coup was in motion.

"It won't be so bad," I said, and "If you'll just give it a *chance*," but too late. The students who weren't still actively protesting had slumped in their chairs. They could still be made to participate, but it would have to be coerced, and participation under duress wasn't really participation at all.

"If you'll just pass these back," I said, handing out the Dover copies.

"Thus do I ever make my fool my purse."

"You are a villain."... "And you—are a senator."

"I hate the moor; and it is thought abroad that 'twixt my sheets he has done my office. I know not if it be true, but for mere suspicion in that kind will do as if for surety."

This was golden stuff, wasn't it? All of the best lines I had looked forward to my students responding to, and they were all sullen and stony faced, as if reading the play was a punishment. They looked out the windows, and slipped their phones partway from their pockets to check for messages. My attendance, after just two days, dropped from a standard ten or fifteen percent of my students missing class to thirty or forty. According to the online grade book, students who were showing up for other parts of the school day were avoiding my room. Most dishearteningly, in my jock section, the class I had *most* envisioned taking off and embracing the material, fewer than half of my students walked through the door on Friday.

I could blame the weather, or post-testing fatigue, or the fact that education, as it was currently practiced in Plains City, didn't prepare students for challenges like reading Shakespeare, but ultimately decided that the things that happened in my classroom really came down to me. I resolved, over the weekend, to redouble my efforts. I would go to bed early on Sunday and arrive Monday morning with fresh vitality. I would review the characters and events of the first two acts with my students, would teach more of the play's vocabulary before my students came across it, and would cast roles more carefully to ensure more lively performances. I would read some of the most difficult speeches aloud myself.

But Monday arrived and my freshened vitality failed to arrive with it. Worse, fewer of my students arrived than had come any day the previous week. Among those who did show, there was a new, malignant difficulty. The whiffs of pot I had smelled intermittently on my students before the break had multiplied and become more pervasive since we'd returned to school. The current I had smelled coming in my windows on the last day of Spring Break now seemed to have been a turning-point: the moment at which marijuana stopped being something I smelled *some* places, *sometimes*, and became something I smelled *always, everywhere.* It was there as soon as I opened my apartment door to set foot in my hallway at the Douglas building each morning; there as soon as I opened the side door of the high school and entered the building. We received administrative emails about it; there were confirmations from law enforcement that we were dealing with a virtually unprecedented uptick in local traffic. A confluence of cultural forces ranging from the messaging of popular music to legalizations in nearby states to the national economic downturn had coalesced to result in more product on the market and more desire for that product. The counselors emailed two and three times a day to share that *So & So,* and also *So & So,* had been caught and were suspended, please send homework to the office. The kids were smoking in their cars before school, in the bathrooms, in the stairwells, and on the theater's balcony. I smelled it on their persons and saw it in their averted glances, hooded lids, and the fine penmanship written into their red-written eyes.

It wasn't just the usual suspects, either. It was also the preps and the jocks, the socs and greasers, the theater kids, band kids, and choir. Activity heads and coaches tried to clamp-down—they threatened removal from their teams—

but the club kids who smoked were casual members, and membership on the spring sports didn't carry the same weight with the kids that the fall and winter ones did. Kids didn't mind being cut from baseball or track.

On the Thursday of the second week back from the break, attendance in my first-block class hit a new low: eleven students from my roster of twenty-eight. While it was tempting to blame the warm weather and the epidemic of smoking pot, I couldn't help but recall my meeting with Mrs. Hirsche first semester and worry that it was The Bard, and that in trying to teach Shakespeare I had carried my Crusade for the Teaching of Real Literature a bridge too far. Perhaps the Head of Literacy had been right, and they *couldn't* do it. Perhaps the stripped-down worksheet-and-short-passage curriculum the administration was implementing was more appropriate for these seventeen-year-old students.

The following Monday, I received and email from Mrs. Kines, the school's head counselor.

Mr. Able,

We've noticed an above-average number of students have begun failing your English II course. As a reminder, the target for all core classes is to keep failure and hold rates below 8%, and you are currently running 22. Do you have plans to work with these students? We in the counseling office would be happy to work with you. Please let us know.

Glancing to the top of the message, I saw that not only Mr. Russel and Mr. Avery, but also Mrs. Hirsche and Mr. Backus were cc'd.

The next day I was ready to finish Shakespeare's play and put the whole experience behind me. I showed up before school and put Act V vocab words and definitions on the board. The warning bell rang, and my students began arriving, then kept coming in. Contrary to the recent trend, the room was more than two-thirds full when the bell rang to start class. Then another student walked in. And another. With better than eighty percent of my students in the room, I would need to catch a number of them up on the first four acts of the play before I could begin with the fifth. Five minutes after the bell there were only three empty seats, and I couldn't remember, for the life of me, who usually occupied them. I would have to go to my computer to look over my electronic roster. As I did so, I half-listened to the jawing in the room, picking up an undercurrent of... what? Antipathy? Rage? It was hard to say. My students who *liked* one another often expressed their affection by talking trash. But no—these were students who *never* spoke to one another—who almost never spoke at all—who were hissing now. Something had happened—an exchange over the weekend. A quantity of money had been traded for a supply of product, and the product had been found to be lacking. Drugs, I figured. Pot, I hoped. "Easy, son," Marcos said, and Edgar Contreras, from the corner of the room, spat back a string of Spanish.

"I'll lay your bitch-ass out," Marcos returned, and I didn't have any choice but to dial the tone of my voice up to 'disciplinary' and call him out.

"Marcos," I said. "Hallway."

"This fool," I heard Javi say as I followed my disgruntled Marcos out of the room. While I first thought he was referring to me, my glance caught Javi jerking his thumb toward the room's back. Now I had a dilemma. My intuition told me I should stay and prevent whatever was about to escalate between Javi and Edgar from escalating, but Marcos was already in the hallway and I was partway out the door following him. I had made a strong commitment to talking to Marcos in the hall; I didn't want to reverse myself.

I shut the door.

"Marcos," I said, and I was relieved to see the big junior's face soften. He had always been reasonable—was secretly a much better student than most of his peers—and I thought I might hear him explain something, that I might say my little piece, and that we could head back in. But the volume in my room came up—there was shouting and the scrape of chair legs on the other side of the door—and I found myself frozen. It wasn't my own impulse so much as the warning look in Marcos's eyes that moved me back into the room.

Inside, half the class was standing and most all of the desks had been displaced. Javi and Edgar occupied an empty space in the middle, the former prancing back and forth hollering his taunts, the latter with his fists and fore-arms up near his cheeks in a way that gave the impression he'd had some boxing training. Javi danced back, danced in, and said, "Fight me, then!" When Edgar stepped forward a moment later and the two collided, there was an almost fake quality to the exchange, as if they were cartoon characters, or playactors. WWF-style imitation wrestlers. Edgar, who had always seemed small, seemed to explode and become larger. Javi expanded and then crumpled like a sheet of loose-leaf paper around him, falling backward to the ground. I wasn't sure, when he hit the floor, that the whole thing wasn't a farce, like when I'd been in school and my friends and I had pretended to slap one another, but really only connected with our own free palms.

It was the sounds my students made—the sickening *Ohhhhh* and the low expletives—and the way so many of them turned to look away—that told me something was really wrong.

"I tol' 'im not to fuck with me," Edgar said as he brushed passed me. "I ain't done nuthin'." He dropped a pair of my classroom scissors to the floor on his way out, a painter's broad red stroke of blood fanning out from one of their blades.

"Somebody call the nurse," I said, kneeling above Javi without knowing how I'd gotten there. I touched his elbow, tried to move his arm away to see how bad the cut was, saw that his shirt was already soaked. "Somebody call 911," I said, my voice rising. "Anybody. Use your cell phones."

19

I couldn't help myself: I spent a great deal of time over the next several days considering ways I might turn the tragedy of a stabbing in my classroom into a "learning opportunity" with tie-ins to *Othello*. I couldn't help but consider Cassio's wounding of Montano during the brawl in the second act of the play, Iago's mortal wounding of Roderigo in act five, and Iago's ice-cold, remorseless slaying of Emilia in the play's final scene.

I had an abundance of time to consider such things because I'd been placed on administrative leave. I wouldn't be permitted to walk back into the building for five school days: the next Thursday at the earliest. Besides the fact it had taken place in my classroom, during my class, the administration wanted to investigate two prominent aspects of Javi's stabbing: the fact that I had stepped out of my room and closed the door to speak with Marcos just before it had happened, and that I had left the assault weapon (the administration's words: *assault weapon*) lying on the back counter of my room for one student to use to assail another.

I explained, in my digitally recorded interview in the

principals' conference room, that in talking to Marcos outside of my room I was following district-provided guidelines I had been given in district trainings: students were more receptive to criticism when they were outside their peers' earshot. With regard to the scissors, I was less equipped to explain myself. I had used them while standing at my back counter to trim some handouts I had made; I hadn't put them away because I had been interrupted by a bell signaling the end of my plan period; I had never thought they might be used by one of my students to *assail* another. As the interview progressed (*What prompted you to return to the room? What did you see when you got back? How did you respond?*) I waited, perhaps stupidly, for the other shoe to drop: why was I teaching *Othello* to begin with? Could the difficulty of the play—or its irrelevance to my students—have stirred them to distraction, antagonism, violence?

But the question never came. It was left for me to ponder in the eerie stillness of my apartment as the daylight and nighttime hours crawled past over the next several days.

Late Thursday afternoon I went downstairs to Wonder's to join my father for coffee. "Did you stop a knife fight in your classroom?" my former student Allison Younger asked across the bakery's counter.

"No," I said. "Scissors."

Her face condensed in a pained way, as if she felt sorry for having to correct me. "Everyone at the school is saying it was a knife."

"It was scissors."

"And Javi's in the hospital? And the other guy's in juvie?"

"Javi's at home. The other kid got OSS."

She nodded, disappointed. "But you pulled him off and broke it up."

"I raised my voice and yelled. It was over before I could get to them."

"Still, though. You were there."

"I was there," I agreed.

I didn't fare much better in speaking with my father.

"You should have talked to me before you gave your deposition," he said at our table a few minutes later. "I could have coached you out of a couple of those statements."

"The truth and nothing but the truth," I said. "I didn't think I had anything to hide."

My father *harumphed* and drank some of his coffee. "When you express feelings of guilt for things that aren't your fault, you open yourself to allegations you don't want to deal with."

"It was my classroom. They were my students."

He *harumphed* again.

I stayed up late that night, slept badly, and didn't get out of bed until practically noon the next day. I managed to talk myself into leaving for a walk an hour later, and when I returned, found my mailbox full to bursting in the Douglas Building's foyer: a cornucopia of bills and bank statements, credit card offers and coupon flyers. There were three large envelopes of a finer quality among the rest: one buff, one navy, and the other a burnished, burnt orange.

The first of these #10 size envelopes bore a return address with the name of a building I recognized from my tenure at the University of Kansas: the home of the law school. I had felt, when I applied, that my chances of getting into KU Law were fairly strong: the school accepted roughly half of its applicants, and my LSAT score was comfortably above the listed median. Stung by the experience of being rejected by so many grad programs four years before, however, I had also prepared myself for the possibility of not being allowed in. Because of the week I'd just had—because I had watched one of my students stab one of my other students; because I wasn't sure if at this time next week I would still have a job after the conclusion of the investigation—this seemed a more likely possibility, and the contents of the envelope in my hand seemed less like a judgement on my worthiness to go to law school and more like a ruling on my worthiness to be a human being permitted to walk the streets of our world. If I didn't get in, I wasn't sure I'd have the strength to walk up the flights of stairs behind me and make it through the door into my apartment. I worked my finger under the flap of the envelope.

Dear Mr. Able, we are pleased to announce...

I was relieved. A tiny morsel of validation after my several weeks' fast. I took my time climbing the stairs and unlocked my door before opening the other two. The first of these was from Ann Arbor; the second, Austin. Sitting on my plaid couch, I found that these, too, were acceptances, each more interesting and enticing than the first. These were acceptances that were competed for. *Sought* after. The sense *their* affirmative answers gave me wasn't just relief or validation, but elation. Receiving them meant I had been *chosen.* As the afternoon advanced, I wondered which of these acceptances I might be more foolish to turn down. I took a walk, watched the sun touch the horizon and turn red. The memory of the blood soaking Javi's white shirt seemed not days but weeks behind, and as the number of blocks between myself and my apartment increased, I understood that I could put not only time but distance between myself and the bleeding disaster my failed teaching career had become. There were doors open for me, heavy and ornate, with wide vistas of opportunity on their other sides.

When I got back to my rooms, I saw that one of the credit card offers I had tossed aside wasn't a credit card offer at all, but a piece of hand-lettered correspondence in a square ivory envelope. Opening it, I found an invitation from Kent and Heidi Lauer to attend the wedding of their daughter Julia to my friend Davis at the end of July. Included was a picture of the couple. They were embracing, standing in front of a house with a stonework façade and soaring windows, a flag standing out straight on its pole— Davis's most recent purchase with his commission money, presumably. His shining red truck was in the circular drive behind them.

I turned over the invitation to examine the particulars, then flipped it over again to look at the picture. *Julia* was marrying Davis. *Davis* was marrying Julia. Dimly, I recognized my confused feelings toward the planned union—that *I* had once been an admirer of Julia's; that, aside from Garret, Davis was the last person I had expected might be leading a settled and successful life before me. My eyes settled on Julia, and a memory of dancing with her at the Club Annabelle flitted across my mind. I recognized the danger I was in. After the last several days alone in my apartment, I wasn't sure even my enviable trio of law school acceptances would be enough to keep me from spiraling. Changing into a pair of jeans and a button-up, I picked up my keys and wallet and made my way downstairs, headed across the way to Dos Amigos to have my dinner at the bar.

20

I was midway through my basket of chips, still waiting for my dinner to arrive, when the leather of the stool next to mine cracked and I looked over to see Jim Jr settling in. He held up a finger and nodded to Arturo, prompting the bartender to retrieve a lowball glass and a squarish bottle of bourbon from one of the higher shelves.

"Been a while," he said by way of greeting.

"Little bit," I agreed.

He asked me what I was drinking, and when I named the cola, he said Arturo's name and told him to pour me a glass of what he was having. "Don't you just live across the street? I never see you in here."

I told him that I did, and that I usually dropped in early for take-out.

"I've been coming in two or three times a week for a while now." He raised his eyes to the game playing on the television behind the bar. "Becoming a bit of an NBA fan. Basketball was your sport, wasn't it?"

He knew it was. I had come in off the bench on varsity as a sophomore, the year he'd been cut at the end of tryouts as a senior. His bringing up my playing struck me as an unusually generous and self-deprecating gesture for him. It made me want to behave more generously toward him. *I did*, I said, and we fell to talking. First my tacos, then a plate of carne asada I hadn't heard him order showed up in front of us. By the time we'd finished eating half an hour later, Denver was twelve points behind and I'd finished a second drink on Jim's tab. He leaned back on his stool.

"Up for a little driving? I know a girl out in Covenant. She's got a couple friends who might be lonely for a guy like you." He sipped his drink. "If you feel like widening your social circle."

I didn't have any plans. Nothing I might have made up on the spot to put him off would have come across as plausible, and, in truth, the prospect of going back up to my apartment and passing the evening alone with my law school acceptances and Davis and Julia's wedding announcement struck me as a sadness I didn't want to contemplate.

"I could meet some people."

Jim asked Arturo to pour a couple of drinks into 'go' cups for us and laid a twenty down on the bar for his trouble. A few minutes later we were in his black Jeep Grand Cherokee heading over the bridge out of town, Jim explaining his satellite radio subscription and pointing out the other features of the vehicle.

The drive was one I had made before, but probably not since high school when drives like it, adventures my friends and I had embarked on to meet up with small town girls we had first met dragging our Main Street or gracing our baseball diamonds, had occasionally enlivened our spring and summer nights. Jim texted as he drove, the screen of his phone illuminating his Jeep's ceiling. I leaned back and let the waves of bass from the woofer beneath the back seat ride through my body and watched the emerging stalks of the spring crops flash by. It began to seem that agreeing to come with him might even have been a good idea. Receiving three acceptance letters to law school had barely been enough to jar me from the funk I had fallen into, and even then a single wedding invitation had caused me to sink again. This might be the kind of outing I needed to gain perspective and buck up.

Twenty-five minutes later Jim hooked a left onto a little dirt culdesac on the edge of Covenant. "It's Mandy, Karissa, and Dani," he said as we got out of the Jeep. "Don't let the dogs jump up on you in the house. They're not allowed."

The red-headed girl who met us at the door surprised me by stepping out and wrapping her arms around Jim's neck, kissing him deeply as the dogs slipped out around her knees. Then she turned and offered me her hand. "Mandy," she said. No sooner had I taken it and told her my own name than was she spinning and disappearing back into the house. "Ge'down, Lacy! Ge'down, Sadie," Jim Jr shouted, and then it was my turn to push the dogs away as I followed him through the door. The front room featured a scratched-up, faux-leather couch covered in dog hair and a chipped entertainment center framing a flatscreen television with bad color balance. There was an open pass-through to what must have been the linoleum-floored kitchen, and doors splitting off to either side: bedrooms. The walls were blank but for a few Polaroid pictures tacked-up, and there were a pair of laundry baskets piled with children's toys at the edge of the floor. It crossed my mind that Jim Jr might have a wife and child he'd been hiding away—then I thought maybe just a child—and then I realized it was more likely he was involved in an affair, that this girl might have a husband somewhere, either working a night shift or deployed overseas, and that by bringing me to this place he had involved me in something illicit and sordid.

"I'm gettin' *ready,*" Mandy called through the door to the left after Jim tried its doorknob and found it locked. Apparently unbothered, he walked back across the room to open its counterpart at the right. On its other side, he began talking.

I weighed the possibility of following him, feared I might be marked unwelcome or intrusive, and decided to sit down on the couch to watch the TV, instead. The moment I did so, Sadie and Lacy jumped up on either side of me to lick my neck and face. I stood back up, and two young women emerged from the room Jim had recently stepped into, one blonde in an undersized t-shirt and cotton shorts, the other brunette in skinny jeans and a tank top. They introduced themselves as the aforementioned Karissa and Dani, each raising a hand by way of greeting, the first with some enthusiasm, the second in a manner more disaffected and perfunctory. I began to say my own name in response, but they were already heading back into the room where I heard, in bits and snatches, Jim Jr begin to tell them about me.

I stood there for the next twenty minutes or so, stroking the dogs' heads and *good girl*ing them until they seemed content to let me sit down in some peace between them, and watched VH1 while the girls yelled back and forth across the house and occasionally crossed before me to retrieve flat irons and bottles of perfume from one another. At one point Dani came out of Mandy's room, picked up a black Bic lighter from beside me on the couch, set a bare foot on the couch's arm, and flicked a flame into being to singe away a thread that had strayed from the seam of her jeans. At another, Jim Jr went into the kitchen and came back with a beer for himself and a second for me. Karissa tried on three different outfits that I saw, conferring with Mandy on two before settling on the third.

"You alright with the Oasis?" Jim Jr leaned out of the girls' room to ask at the end of these proceedings.

I told him that the Oasis sounded fine to me.

"Able wants to go to the Oasis," he called over his shoulder. "Let's just go there."

Over the din of a hair dryer and the shutting of a closet, I heard both girls call back their agreement, and a moment later Dani came into the room holding up a shimmering black sequined top she hadn't finished strapping on yet.

"Help me with this?"

"Sure." I stood up as she stepped in close to me and turned. Her recent activities in getting ready had enveloped her body in heat, and the cumulative effect of this heat with the fragrances of her shampoo, body lotion, deodorant, and perfume was heady—impossible to parse or total. "Is it—" I began to ask, and she lifted her hair, making clear what I needed to help her with: a pebble-sized glass bead needed to slip through a tiny cloth loop. I pinched the little bead, tried and failed to avoid the intimacy of grazing the skin at the back of her neck, and slipped it through its eyelet. "There."

"Thank you." The curtain of her hair fell back into place and she skipped back into her bedroom.

In my personal first-impression short-hand, Mandy seemed sweet and wholesome, Karissa ditzy, but at least self-awarely so, and Dani aloof and cynical, reminiscent of the kinds of jaded girls I sometimes had in class who were smart but disdained being seen as so. Ten minutes after I'd helped Dani with her bead and eyelet, the five of us were tumbling out the door and piling into Jim's Jeep, screaming back down the road toward Plains City and the Oasis.

At the club's door Efrain Sanchez, a former two-year member of my study hall, now one of the establishment's venerable bouncers, clapped me on the shoulder and said "Nice work, Mr. A," as Jim and the girls passed through. We made our way through the crowd to a table adjacent to the bar's 'perv row' looking over the dance floor, and I was greeted by not just two or three, but four or five different former students. Before we had finished settling, Camilla was in waiting at my shoulder, saying "Evening, Will," and asking what it was our table wanted to drink. After she'd gone, Dani narrowed her eyes.

"Why do all these kids know you?"

I didn't point out that some of these *kids* were probably only two or three years younger than her. "I was their teacher," I said. "I teach at the high school."

Her eyes narrowed further. She turned to Jim. "I thought you said he was going to law school."

"*Going to go*. I said he was *going to go*. Not that he was already there. Able's just passing some time at the high school now. It's like a Teach for America thing. Charity. But don't kid yourself, he's gonna bill three times as much as me, easy." He turned to face me. "You're going to KU in the fall, right?"

To his disappointment, I shook my head. "I got into KU, but I don't think I'm going to go. Right now I'm trying to decide between Michigan and Texas, and I have a few other applications I'm still waiting to hear back on."

Jim Jr's heavy eyelids rose. "Those are good fucking schools." He turned to face the girls. "Those are really good fucking schools."

Around the table, I could see the way this intelligence

shifted the girls' opinions of me. In particular, the skepticism so recently apparent on Dani's face disappeared as if air-brushed away. She steepled her fingers, and a few minutes later I felt the arch of a shoe-shorn foot rub against my ankle beneath the table. She didn't look at me as this happened, but inclined her head toward mine and smiled as a new topic of conversation was introduced by Karissa. I didn't move my own foot towards her, but I didn't move it away, either. A minute later Camilla showed up to hand us our drinks.

The night accelerated. We finished one round of drinks, ordered another, and, after spending a few songs on the dance floor, asked Camilla to bring us a third. Ten o'clock became ten-thirty, and ten-thirty became eleven. The hoped-for crowd at the Oasis failed to materialize.

"We should get out of here," Mandy complained, and "This place sucks," Dani agreed. The girls began to debate whether we should head to Kemper's, the Triple-B, or The Wheel.

"Fuck that," Jim said. "I've got everything any of you could want back at my place, and a hot tub to boot."

This got the girls' attention.

"I could do that," Mandy said, and Karissa and Dani agreed. The matter was decided.

We passed a line of shoe-polished cars and rusted trucks on our drive down River Road, and then the sagebrush retreated and the appearance of carefully-kept Kentucky Bluegrass at the road's edge announced the club's entrance. Taking the left at the second fork, we circled around toward the darkness of the back nine.

In the shuffle leaving the bar, Mandy had taken my former seat in the front and I had slipped into the Jeep's second row behind Jim. Dani was straddling the low rise of the inside 'bitch' seat, sliding in toward me. Certain trajectories for the night felt to be firming up, and it seemed possible and even likely the two of us might end up sleeping together. I felt keenly the competing notions that I would like for this to happen and that I would likely regret it in the morning if it did. Best, probably, to not sleep with her, I thought, but I had a keen sense memory of my fingers grazing her neck as I had slipped that little bead through its loop two hours before. The idea that there might be a symmetry in my slipping it back out later was powerfully appealing.

Jim Jr pulled up a steep drive, pressed a garage door-opener in the visor above his forehead, and parked in a startlingly white garage. His kitchen had similar flooring and cabinetry to my father's, with lighter wood and darker tiles. To our bunched gathering near the fridge he offered cans of beer and glassfuls of bourbon, vodka, wine, and rum.

The back door opened to reveal the patio and promised hot tub with its pair of umbrella-shaped propane lamps. There was the golf course beyond his railing, and in scanning some of the lights on the far side I thought I could pick out my father's, a little higher on the highest rise than the rest.

"Are you sure it's hot enough?" Karissa asked. The night's chill had been evident since we'd left the girls' place. Here, exposed to the wind on Jim's back porch, the temperature verged on cold.

"She's pretty steady," Jim said. He pointed to the propane heaters. "And I'll get these cranked up. Able, you wanna grab some towels?" He told me of a bathroom closet inside and down the hall.

I made my way in, looking through open doorways and checking out Jim's mostly empty rooms as I searched for the bathroom. One of them had only his framed law school diploma leaning against the wall, another a bed, dresser, and standing mirror. In the bathroom at the end of the hall I gathered an armful of turquoise towels (his mother's purchase, or something lifted from his parents' house, I assumed), and turned to find Dani at my elbow.

"Need some help?"

There was a suggestive ambiguity about the question. "Sure," I said after a moment had stretched out. She took the stack from me and set it on the counter, stepping into the space the towels had occupied. Her arms fell around my shoulders, and for the second time of the evening, my fingertips grazed the back of her neck. I smelled and then tasted the rum on her breath; felt her tongue press against and between my teeth.

"Y'all need some help with those?" someone—Karissa— asked. We parted and I picked up the towels. Karissa led us back outside.

Some JL speakers set up on an acrylic table were playing a popular R&B song we had heard earlier at the bar, and Jim and Mandy were negotiating the degree to which the latter ought to disrobe. Entirely, was Jim's position, but Mandy thought it would be more appropriate to keep her under-wear on. "There's other people here," she argued.

"Nothing they ain't seen before," Jim grunted back. "Well, Able, maybe." His laugh echoed out into the night. He had taken his own shirt off, and now stood holding the loosed tongue of his belt idly in one hand. Beside him, the flames beneath the two propane umbrellas fanned out blue-red-orange-yellow and the tub burbled.

"We just doin' our skivvies, then?" Karissa asked.

"Whatever floats your boat."

Jim stepped out of his khakis, and Mandy and Karissa

began bending and twisting to shuck the clothes they had spent so much time putting on earlier. I set the towels down on the table and watched with a sense of missed opportunity as Dani stretched one of her arms back to release her bead from its loop.

"Oh, it's hot!" Karissa squealed as she slipped over the tub's edge into the water. "Y'all comin' in?"

I dropped my own pants and unbuttoned my shirt, felt first the night's chill, then the heat of the propane umbrellas as I passed beneath them. The water was like embers at first, and then I felt my body acclimate, the currents swirling like nipping fish around me. Dani splashed in and entangled one of her arms with mine, and I slipped down neck-deep to tilt my head back on the rest.

Even here, in this dark corner of the country club in empty Western Kansas, the light pollution from Jim Jr's house and the homes of his neighbors' washed out most of the stars. The tub's pumps rumbled and the water circulated. Jim boasted about his plans for his house, answering the girls' questions as they asked them, and then peppered them in turn with his own questions about their tattoos and how soon they would be dropping various articles of clothing over the tub's edge.

"What's in it for us," Mandy wanted to know.

"Quid pro quo," Jim said, causing Karissa to crinkle her nose. "Tit for tat," he said to clarify. Then, furrowing his brow, "Tits..."—but he couldn't come up with any wordplay to finish the joke.

Some of the tension I'd been carrying in my neck having melted away, I sat up and looked at my tubmates. Condensation and sweat were beading on everyone's faces and shoulders. The steam was making Dani's hair curl in a tight and attractive way. I found that since we'd debarked from the

Jeep, the arguments on both sides of the internal debate I'd been having about her had been strengthened. I wanted both more to sleep with her and felt increasingly sure I wouldn't be happy with myself if I did. A vocabulary word from my class came to the forefront of my mind: *ambivalent*, from the prefix *ambi-*, suggesting "both," and the root *valent*, meaning "capacity" or "power." If I was in school, I would explain the word by first referencing the term *ambidextrous*, which most of my students would know—or understand, at least, after I had explained it to them—and then comparing *ambivalent* to a word it was often confused with: *indifferent*. To be *indifferent* was to not care. To be *ambivalent* was to care strongly in two opposing directions: to be drawn apart by two great competing *capacities*, or torn between two great *powers*.

You might be indifferent *about lunch, in which case you wouldn't care whether you had a hot dog or a hamburger,* I would explain. *But you might be* ambivalent *about who to invite to Prom, if, say, you really enjoyed talking to so-and-so in your algebra class, but so-and-so in social studies always made you laugh and you thought there might be potential for a future there.*

In our burbling cauldron, Dani's fingers tangled with mine, squeezed. I lifted my arm out of the water and settled it around her shoulder. She floated in close to me.

Why should I feel ambivalent about pursuing some kind of romantic end to the evening? I wasn't puritanical—did, in fact, read and teach authors who were critical of the Puritans and their puritanism. And it wasn't like I would be making an unwelcome advance—the woman beside me was the one who was, so far, making all of the advances. The small knot of her shoulder fitted like an apple into my palm, I reviewed my possible motivations: the fact that I had had a terrible week; my jealousy of Davis's impending nuptials with Julia; my lingering confusion and insecurity about the entire situation with Kelsey Pomerantz over Christmas break two and a half months before; the fact that my attraction to Dani was rooted almost entirely in her being attractive—*hot*—equipped with the type of body that had won twenty-something starlets lead roles in sitcoms, romantic comedies, and horror movies throughout the history of television and film. The fact I might merely be interested in her because she was *available,* because Jim had advertised her and her friends earlier, as we drove out to Covenant, as "girls who would love to get down with you," so that by sleeping with her I might actually be fulfilling Jim Jr's expectations of me instead of my own... I felt her hand slip off my knee and down inside my thigh, and none of these possible motivations seemed particularly damning.

Weren't these perfectly good reasons that I, an available man, might sleep with her, an available woman? Perfectly fine reasons for letting things take their course? Didn't I *deserve* physical affection? And shouldn't I accept succor if it was being offered? Wouldn't it be rude to deny what physical affection and succor I might be able to offer in return to someone who had their own needs and desires? Why be an ascetic?

"I don't give a fuck," Dani said, laughing.

I wasn't paying attention—didn't know the context of the conversation—but felt her last word as much as I heard it; saw it roll over the water and take the place of *Ambivalent* on the mental white board of my mind. *Fuck.* As in, *Dani and I could* fuck. Or: *Why not fuck?* Or: *Why the fuck not fuck?* Or: *To sleep with Dani might be a spectacular way to fuck up.* This word was both more simple than *ambivalent* and more complex. Sophisticated. *Multivalent*: loaded with many powers and capacities. A word that could be noun, verb, adverb, or adjective; a person, action, expletive, or intensifier. I moved my hand down into the water, found small purchase at her side. She slid her hand up my leg, squeezed. Dani and I could *fuck* in multiple ways, *multivalently*. I felt myself becoming less ambivalent and simply *valent*, drawn more powerfully toward her and a particular way the night might end.

Jim waved his hand in front of my face and then pointed. "There's still some good lots with fairway views around the way," he said. "You could talk to your dad about getting a loan. When you're done with school we could be neighbors."

The implication of his speech was clear: tonight didn't have to be a one-time thing. Nights like this with Mandy, Karissa, and Dani could be a regular occurrence. We could take more trips to the bar, host barbecues, have hot tub time not just with these three girls, but others. I might sleep with Dani tonight and Karissa sometime down the road. Mandy, maybe. Jim Jr and I wouldn't just be coworkers, but social collaborators. Friends. Jim Jr might become my best friend. "I'm actually not sure if I'm even going to go, yet," I said.

"No?" Dani's hand drifted back toward my knee. Her face floated into my field of vision and she scrutinized me.

"What are you going to do?" Jim wanted to know.

This was the reason I shouldn't sleep with Dani. The fact that her attraction to me was rooted in an untruth: the idea that I was going to law school; the notion that I would someday be a lawyer—presumably a rich one. It would be fucking under false pretenses: *lying to* to *lie with*. And it wasn't that I *knew* that I didn't want to be a lawyer, but that sleeping with her now seemed tantamount to making the decision. That sleeping with her would mean I had *decided* to be a lawyer, and that the reason I had decided was that doing so would allow me to sleep with—to *fuck*—hot, twenty-something party girls.

"I'm thinking about staying in the classroom to teach," I said, floating out the test balloon as much for Dani and Jim Jr as myself. In the air, it didn't sound so terrible to me, but Dani seemed to find it less attractive. Her body rose on a current of hot water and drifted a few inches away. My hand slipped off her side, came back to my own. As if to fill some of the space her friend had vacated, Karissa leaned forward. "I used to want to be a teacher!"

"Did you?"

"When I was in grade school and middle school." She rose part-way out of the water and looked off, as if pensively. One of her hands came up to move a wet rope of hair back over her shoulder, and her breasts rose up cupped in their brassiere as if with their own buoyancy. In combination, her words and the gesture struck me as profoundly, transparently false. Enticing as the prospect of playing along was, I couldn't bring myself to give her sincerity the benefit of the doubt. "It's an awful job," I said flatly.

"Yeah, but don't you—"

"The kids, the parents, the principals. They're all—" I heard the beginning of my old refrain and I stopped. It was a complaint I had already aired too often, for too long. A lesson I was teaching as if by rote, automatically, instead of with real authenticity. I didn't want to say it again—didn't want to hear myself say it again. I wasn't only offended by it, but bored. Around the tub, the other four gazed at me like intrigued pupils. "There's just so much potential," I said at last. "And it's all just leaking away." There was a little 9-volt charge behind my nose. My vision went fuzzy.

"You *should* teach," Karissa said. "They *need* you."

They *needed* me? This was too much. Tits-forward, it was too clear she was patronizing me and trying to ginny up some kind of shallow romantic connection. Even if she was sincere in thinking the kids did *need* me, her expression of it demonstrated how simple, stupid, and shallow her grasp of the profession was. I recalled standing near Mrs. Bryant, my former Algebra teacher, at her retirement reception two years before when one our fellow teachers walked up to fawningly chastise her. *No one can teach algebra like you, Mrs. Bryant. You're robbing the school of its best math teacher if you leave.*

Mrs. Bryant's anger had surprised me then, but I understood it now. *I've done my time,* she'd snarled back. *Let somebody else take their turn.*

I turned from Karissa to Jim. "Is that why you went into law?" I asked. "Because the law needed you?"

Jim chuckled his cruel, negating chuckle. "Nope."

"That's why you get to charge by the hour," I said bitterly. "Everybody needs teachers, so we have to do it practically for free."

Jim squinted. "That doesn't make any sense."

"It doesn't," I agreed. I stood up, lifted a leg over the tub's edge.

"It's chlorinated, dude. You can piss in the water."

I was already out, my feet slapping the cold boards of the deck. I began to pull on my pants, fighting to stretch them over my wet legs and soaked boxer shorts. I stretched on my undershirt, pulled on my socks and shoes.

"You coming back in, or are we done here?" Jim asked, and I considered the rectangle of yellow light coming through the glass pane of his back door, calculated how much distance going through his house and taking the back road around the club might add to my journey.

"I'm taking off," I said over my shoulder. I began descending the elevated porch's back staircase to the yard below.

"Aw, c'mon. These girls are about to get naked. No need to get all emotionally drunk."

My feet found the concrete slab at the bottom of the stairs, and I stepped off into the grass. There was doubtless a gate somewhere, but by country club rule Jim's privacy fence only came up to my waist, anyway. I crossed his lawn to the closest place where I could meet with it, set my hands on the rough-cut top, and climbed over.

"There we *go*! They're doing it! Will, get back up here, man!" There was a peal of laughter, and "*Will-iam*" and "*Wi-lliam*" I heard two of the girls, Karissa and Mandy, I thought, call out. Stalks of grass and sagebrush still winter-dead brushed against my ankles and legs. I high-stepped and lifted my hands to maneuver through.

"*Gonna miss out!*" Jim bellowed. "*Stand up and show him!*" I cleared the rough and made it to the three-inch grass at the fairway's margin, heard the girls' laughter and the splashes they made falling back into the tub as I did so.

21

The sounds of the revelry taking place in the hot tub behind me receded as I moved onto the fairway. I crossed a spar of rough and oriented myself to cross the course at an angle I thought would take me toward my father's. The most direct route home to my apartment would pass by there and through part of the Hackshaw Preserve on my way toward the river. In the middle of the thirteenth hole, the night seemed to get darker, the stars above me to stand out a little more sharply, and then as I neared the lake in the middle of the course with its spotlights on the course's windmill, brightness began to wash out the night sky again. I was still angry as I passed this midpoint—I was moving under the power of my anger— and then as I approached the more populated side of the club where my father and his neighbors lived, I slowed to a stop, considering how ridiculous I might appear to someone who chanced to be out on their back porch or looking out their window and saw me. Why had I done this? Perhaps I was, as Jim Jr had suggested, "emotionally drunk."

Some of the heat of my anger abated, and I gained a

clearer sense of the temperature. It hadn't only seemed cold on Jim's porch because we'd stripped out of our warm clothes. A north wind was blowing and it actually *was* cold. Fixing to get colder still. I needed to keep moving.

While some of the lights a few houses down from my father's were on, the lights at his own were off, and I hewed near to it as I left the grass surrounding the fourth hole's putting green. There was a barbed wire fence separating the club from the buffalo preserve; I wrapped both my hands around its top wire and pressed down, lifting one leg over, then the other. That I caught my pants and cut my trail leg —deep enough to draw blood—was proof I was either more intoxicated than I had thought or a great deal less agile than I'd been the last time I'd done this at the age of nineteen.

"Fuck," I said, an expression of pain. Then, gritting my teeth: "I don't give a *fuck*."

I looked over my shoulder. I was, I thought, far enough from my father's not to be heard. "I don't give a fuck," I repeated, testing the sound of my voice in the air.

Fuck: a noun this time. Synonymous with "care," as in *I don't give a care.* An idiomatic way of expressing the more straight-forward *I don't care.*

If the statement passed my volume test, it failed my check for truth. Because I did care, didn't I? Whether or not I was heard; what people thought of me. Cared what I did with my life. Cared about teaching.

This was what had set me off in the hot tub—the twin arguments implicit in Karissa's *You should teach! They need you!*: that, since I was thinking about leaving teaching, I didn't *care*; that I should teach because the kids were in need of *care*taking.

The lights of the club had disappeared behind me. I pulled out my phone, opened it, and pushed the 'send' button to light up its screen, sweeping it back and forth like a low-watt flashlight. I came to a small stream and stepped over it onto a kind of broad flat. Walking between some low cacti I found myself confronted by a pair of unlikely boulders. "Why should it be up to me to care?" I asked. One of the boulders turned to me and snorted, its giant eye shining. I recalled my students who continued talking after the bell had rung, the ones who came in ten and fifteen minutes late, who came in reeking of pot, who put their heads down before I even began speaking... The problem wasn't that *I* didn't care. It was that no one else did. "Why should I care if they don't?" I asked. The near buffalo—because that's what these boulders were, buffalo—turned its head to regard me. "The problem isn't that *I* don't care," I explained. "It's that I care too much. The problem is that they've left all the caring up to me."

The other buffalo snorted, swung its head my way. I backed away.

I could veer back to the north toward the country club and the highway—which would mean backtracking at least half a mile—or walk east toward the river, reaching it at a point farther south than I had intended and walking its sandy bottom like a highway that would lead me eventually to the bridge a few blocks from my apartment window. I decided on this latter course, walked east.

My route took me across the northern panhandle of the irregularly shaped preserve. I successfully squeezed between the wires of another section of the fence without cutting myself and made my way down a steep decline to the bottom of an elbow of the river I hadn't seen since I was seventeen and several of my friends and I had passed a summer afternoon exploring on four wheelers and an ATV. I shivered and then yawned, felt my buzz wearing thin.

Town, I realized, was still much farther off than I'd expected it to be after so much walking. How far had I made it since leaving Jim Jr's? Two miles? Three? And how far did I have still to go? Three miles? Four? The bank on the far side of the sandy riverbed was higher here, screening the view and even the glow of the city from sight. It seemed as if Plains City might not be there at all—that I ran the risk of becoming lost in the cold and still-cooling darkness. I probably should have stayed and taken my chances with Dani or Karissa; sacrificed my integrity to get my rocks off and enjoy the pleasure of a warm bed with a warm person sleeping beside me.

I began to hear a dull, distant pulse, like the early phases of a community college party starting above my apartment. So strong was my sense of this that I caught myself looking up, as if my apartment ceiling might be there. Even after I'd assured myself it wasn't, for the next dozen paces I was sure that I was closer to home than I had thought—close enough to hear the community college kids' music. Then I began to hear voices, and remembered the line of cars and trucks Jim Jr and the girls and I had seen as we had driven out earlier from the Oasis. Some of the high school kids must have stayed out to continue their river party after curfew. I slowed my pace, afraid they might see me before I could see them. A rap song popular with the kids was playing, ended, and the next song that came on turned out to be country. As when DJ Saucedo played at the Oasis, the kids' musical choices tilted toward an eclectic collective taste.

Soon I made out the kids' bonfire's glow, and began to see the loose circle of trucks and jeeps that some of them had driven down nearer to the river's bed. I began to pick out people, first in clumps, then standing apart from one another on the bed's roadside bank. I would almost certainly be seen if I maintained my course walking down the bed's center, or even if I moved to the far side. I crossed to the opposite bank and made my way up onto it. The far bank was higher than the roadside one. When I came even with the party I stopped and looked down on it from my privileged vantage.

A surprising number of teenagers had defied curfew to be hangers-on and risk arrest by the sheriffs. Among a number of youths I didn't have in class, I saw a veritable who's-who of my most indifferent and apathetic students, and a number of my so-called 'average' and even very good ones, too. Here were kids who seldom showed up and who slumped in their chairs when they did alongside students who regularly did the readings and raised their hands to participate. Here were the kids who set the curve talking and dancing with kids who, stoned, wouldn't have bothered to try to copy the work off another's paper and cheat to get by. Two of my most chronically absent, Carson Villanueva and Dalton Erickson, were near enough to the river's bank with a pair of their friends that I could hear their conversation:

"I shit you not. I'm being so fucking for real right now," said the former.

"The fuck you are," contended the latter, tossing the glowing stub of whatever he was smoking down into the river. "Let's go then."

"Nah. I don't wanna knock you out."

"If you say so."

They came close to one another and tussled.

"Bitch. Don't make me—"

"Ow! Fucker!"

Their shadows came apart, and one fell into the sandy bed of the river.

"I'm drunk, fool. If I wasn't, you'd—"

I backed away, moving deeper into the brush. I had received emails about both of the combatants in the last week. Both were on the principals' watchlist. Carson was a junior more than five classes behind schedule, and Dalton was a senior taking my junior-level English class concurrently with the sophomore-level one in hopes of making up credit and graduating. Neither was on track to pass. These were the students who spent the least amount of time in my class, about whom I spent a disproportionate amount of time exchanging emails with counselors and administrators, who cared not at all, and about whom I was supposed to care. And care and care and care.

And that was the thing. I wasn't *just* supposed to be a teacher, but a social worker—or surrogate parent. To deal with student A's irresponsibility and B's misbehavior. C, D, and E's substance abuse problems, F's dyslexia and G's anger. H's lack of faith in herself, I and J's sureness that what I was offering wasn't for them. K and L's insecurity about their weight, M and N's eating disorders. O's male body image issues, P, Q, and R's confusions about their sexuality. Autistic S's frustrations about his inability to understand social norms and cues. T's anger at the rest of the class slowing her education down; U's bullying, V's being bullied. W and X being sure their athletic prowess would carry them through life (it wouldn't), and Y and Z's inability to stay awake in class because they were working too many hours outside of school to help their parents make ends meet. For every kid I had in a stable, two-parent household, another was a child of divorce—if their parents were ever married to begin with. A *hated* her stepmother, B was hated by his. Social Services had removed C from her home because her stepfather couldn't stop touching her, and D had written three essays about how his family only adopted him for the paycheck. And so I wanted to care (*and care and care*), but had to contend with the administrators and *their* nonsense, and had my own life to live, as well. It was stretching me too thin. I was suffering compassion fatigue, and, compounding this, decision fatigue. And I wanted to be *fair*, but what was fair? "Treating everyone the same isn't the same as treating everyone fair," the counselors had told us. So *of course* I would accommodate E by shortening the reading home-work, and F by striking every fourth distractor from each of my multiple-choice questions. I would lessen the strain on G by providing a fill-in-the-blank organizational template for each of her papers, and facilitate H's success by providing him with extra time for each and every assign-ment, and I by finding an audio version of everything that we read in class. J, the counselors had made clear, should *never* get extra time, but should always have her assign-ments shortened by 33 percent. And after fulfilling all of these state-mandated accommodations, shouldn't I fudge just a little for K, L, M, and N, who clearly had needs but weren't born to the kind of parents who had the resources, time, or wherewithal to make the noise necessary to get their kids the help they deserved? *Won't you, just once*, Mrs. Kines, the head counselor, wanted to know. *If at all possible*, read the myriad parent emails. *O and P are on the watchlist*, Mr. Avery's emails began.

...*and care and care and care and care.* And then to be subject to patronizing treatment—*You have to! They need you!*—as if this *caring* was a sort of payment, virtue as its own reward, and not, in fact, a type of fee, or toll, taxing me and drawing me down, winnowing away my strength and spirit.

Why should I care? Why carry (*care-y?*) so many of soci-

ety's burdens—and suffer a social penalty for doing so?
Girls like Kelsey Pomerantz slummed with me, and Dani, on
hearing I might continue to teach instead of going to law
school, had slid away from me in the hot tub's waters.
Shouldn't I be making money, like Davis, who would marry
Julia? Wasn't stupid, sleazy Jim Jr floating high surrounded
by bare tits and ass miles behind me, like a king?

My foot caught on a tuft of grass anchored in the sand
and I stumbled, hit the ground. Rising and dusting myself
off, I looked back and decided I was far enough away from
the high schoolers that none of them could have seen or
heard me. I edged back down toward the river's bed, stepped
back into it, and continued on my way, coming upon the
mound.

It was one of those immense anthills, I thought at first,
like you sometimes see in the pages of National Geographic,
or on documentaries. Almost as tall as I was and five or six
feet wide, decorated all over with rocks and bits of metal
and glass. Some kind of mounded-up throne the kids had
made, I realized. So they could choose a king or queen for
their river parties. Someone sat atop it and declaimed and
pronounced things. I pulled out my phone to make use of its
dim light to better examine it... and saw a framed picture of
Bryce: a glossy 5x9 of him in his football pads, kneeling,
helmet on the ground beside him, on the school field's
twenty-five-yard line. Someone must have pulled it out of
one of the trophy cases by the gym. Here were bottles of Bud
Light and Budweiser, Coors Light and Coors Heavy, Natty
Lite, Mickey's, Olde English, Aftershock and various stripes
of Schnapps, too. Jack Daniels and Johnny Walker. Barton's
Vodka and McCormick's gin. Seagram's rum and Jose
Cuervo tequila. I looked off in the direction where I knew
the road to run, and knew I must be about even with the

place his truck had finished rolling. It wasn't a throne, but a memorial. A monument. A shrine.

There was the charge again, behind my nose, as in the hot tub but more powerful, and my tears came out freely. I cried for a few minutes, wiped my snot away on my sleeve, and then pinched back the last of my tears. Picking up the tarnished frame, I shined my phone's light onto the picture. Bryce was, in it, somehow both older and younger than I expected him to be, but entirely himself. The eight-year-old boy I had discovered on waking after a night of high school pranking, who I had capered around with on my back. The kid I had played "horse" with and tossed a football to, who I'd snuck into the student section of high school games in the fall and who had cheered for me in the winter. Who had been my *student* before he was my student, and then had become the most important student in my class. You could see it in the way his smiling lips pulled back to reveal his teeth. He was here, and now he was gone. What was this quintessence of dust?

Bryce hadn't cared, not really. Not at first. But he had *deserved* to care, and he had *learned* to care. He had, because I had cared about him, cared about me. And he'd led others to caring.

There was the revving of an engine, a whoop and a holler. I turned and saw headlights sweep across some of the higher ground behind me on the far side of the river. Setting the framed picture back into its place, I crouched and ran toward the road-side of the riverbed where I squatted, waiting for a pair of headlights that never came. After a few minutes, I stood back up and continued my walk.

Had I really cared? Had I really *tried* caring? Or was caring at the forefront of my mind because it was my most prized currency, the one I was most reluctant to spend? I had cared about *Shakespeare*, certainly. And a lot of good that had done me. But then, Shakespeare was the subject matter I wanted to teach. *There are 'student' teachers and there are 'content' teachers*, Lauren West had said. *You're clearly the latter.*

Caring about the students was different than caring about the content. And maybe, I had to admit, harder. A broader and more encompassing task. Had I really tried caring about them? Or had I merely *affected* caring about them—*faked* caring about them, putting on a show—because fake caring greased the wheels and made the job of delivering my content easier? I had been a clever teacher, but had I been a good one? And if I hadn't, could I be?

The foliage became taller and more dense—impassable —and I strayed closer to the road, veering away from the river. After a time I came to the highway and, when I saw no headlights, hurried across it. I would move fifty or a hundred yards into the stretch of plain on its other side, then, I thought, into a swath of ground I had seen from my distant apartment window but had never been on, and on it I would cut to the east, cross the river near the fair grounds, and then skirt the rodeo arena and be almost home.

I walked. I had cared *sometimes,* I decided. *Often,* even. But I doubted I had done so *consistently*. Would it make a difference if I *had*? If I *did*? Maybe quitting and going to law school wasn't the answer. Maybe staying and doubling-down on caring was. It wouldn't be easy, but...

It came to me that I was caught, for the second time in the last few hours, in a powerful ambivalence, whipped between being all but sure that I wanted leave and wash my hands of the profession—and plunging myself in from toes to crown, immersing myself. Whipped so hard and fast as to feel I hadn't moved at all—had somehow remained in the same place despite the tremendous distance I had traveled. The force of it threatened to rip me in two.

To teach, or not to teach? That was the question, and the simultaneous urgency and futility of it gave me sudden insight into the play I had finished reading in my living room so recently without feeling I had understood it at all. "Hesitancy" wasn't a strong enough word to describe Hamlet's tragic flaw. Neither was "Indecision." It was a vicious, mind-tearing *ambivalence*. A terminal case of *paralysis*. Hamlet suffered the worst fate an actor could suffer in a staged play, perhaps the worst thing that could happen to any of us in life: he suffered his *failure to act*. And it was rooted in... A failure to know himself? A fear of behaving wrongly? An overdeveloped capacity for thinking?

I stared up. The darkness was more complete here, the stars more bright. A line came to me: *We live in the flicker.* Was that *Hamlet*? Or *Macbeth*? Something else altogether? Whatever the root of Hamlet's trouble was, I wasn't sure that knowing it myself mattered. The play's argument was against this indecisive waffling. The key was *to be*—to *act*. I couldn't remain ambivalent forever. I needed to choose. Whether to be a teacher, a lawyer, or someone else entirely, I needed to choose *my* life. Life was, as my student Bryce had taught me, preciously short. Wouldn't it be better to choose a life now about which I cared? This was almost certainly the case. I might now be ready for such a life, I thought. And wasn't it the readiness, as the play had suggested, that was all?

22

"Okay, so what did we learn?"

It was Thursday. I had been cleared of wrongdoing the day before and come back to find my classroom pitiably empty. Not of students, but of life. Indeed, I had more of my students in their desks now than I had had during any other day save the first one since Spring Break, but they themselves were much less present. Javi was back, but silent. Edgar had been suspended. Marcos, Adrienne, and a couple of the others were looking up at me stoically, as if ready and willing to suffer whatever punishment it was they knew they deserved, and the rest of the class was looking down at their desks and the floor, or askance at the windows and door.

There was entirely too much contrition in the room; it wouldn't do. We needed to move past it.

I had thought, in the last few days, about scrapping my *Othello* unit. Turning the page, so to speak: starting something fresh to get a fresh start on the last stretch of the semester. But I found when I thought about this that we had worked too hard to throw the unit away without any concluding remarks, and quitting something unfinished set a bad precedent—not the kind of thing I wanted to do even at this late juncture of the school year; not the kind of example I wanted to set for my students.

"It's not about what I learned," I said. "It's about what you got out of the play. When you walk out of here, what is it you're going to take with you from *Othello*?"

A few more of them looked up, but no one spoke. Javi slid the book from side to side on his desk. Adrienne opened her copy and made a show of turning its pages. Ruefully, I thought that if I'd had this silence two weeks ago, I might have passed through the unit without incident.

"We'll make it a small group question," I said. "Turn and ask your neighbor what they learned. You and your neighbor will chat for two minutes, then you'll turn to talk to the pairing that is either right in front or right behind you."

I checked the clock, uncapped my marker, made note of the time two minutes hence on the board. "You may begin."

As I watched, some life came back to the room. Conversations reluctantly began, picked up steam, and then sputtered and died. The class again became silent. "Now turn and talk with your partner pairings," I said, and the choking-and-dying engine process repeated itself. "And that's time," I said after the time expired. The room had already fallen back to silence.

"So what happened in the play?" I caught a flicker of an eye. "Marcos?"

"Dude killed his wife." Marcos intoned in his basso profundo.

"How do we feel about that?"

He shrugged. "It's messed up."

This was an answer I could work with. "Do we all agree?

That Othello murdering Desdemona is *messed up*? Or are there other opinions?"

A few shaking heads. "Is it Desdemona's fault? Does she deserve this?"

More shaking heads. Marcos spoke again for the class. "No sir."

"So whose fault is it?"

"Iago." This voice was higher, brighter. Javi.

"Iago," I echoed, looking around. Other students were nodding. "Othello's the one who smothered his wife, though, isn't he? Are we saying it was Iago's fault?"

"Iago did him dirty," Javi said. "Dude tricked him."

"He might have tricked him, but strangling someone to death..." I paused, held up my hands, let the image of an imaginary neck take root in my students' minds. "Can a person *make* another person do that?"

Some uneasy and sideways glances. I heard a few muttered asides, students airing their opinions privately to neighbors, but no one spoke before the class. "This is an important question. Who's more at fault, Othello or Iago?"

A number of voices, now. Adrienne Gallegos's rang out above them all. "Men in general," she said. This earned some smiles from fellow women and scowls from several of the young men.

"I'm not sure Emilia would disagree with you. But if we consider that the play is called *Othello*, and that it's a tragedy, is it a tragedy because Othello succumbs—fails—through faults of his own, or because he's tricked and manipulated by Iago?" Another swell and fall of student voices, this one, too, inconclusive.

"Let me ask the question a different way. Who is the main character—the *protagonist*—of the play? Is it Othello, or Iago?"

Several students named Othello.

"Do you think Othello has control over his own life?"

No answer.

"Do you guys have control of yours?"

A few eyes widened, as if burgeoning with response, but no one spoke.

"Here's what I'm getting at. The play isn't called *Iago*, or *Desdemona*. It's called *Othello*, and it's a tragedy. Since it's a tragedy, I think we can safely say it's a tragedy about a tragic hero named Othello. And per the tragic formula we talked about at the beginning of the unit, the downfall has to be the tragic hero's own fault. His own *damn* fault, because the word *damn* means to judge, and is strongly associated with God's judgement, and when we read a *tragedy, we* should judge the hero so that we can learn from their mistakes. And avoid them."

I paused. "Do we agree on this premise? That Othello is the protagonist of the play? And that he has a flaw that we should learn from? Because I'm willing to discuss the question. It has something to do with a conversation we had first semester, when we talked about grammar. Subjects and objects. Subjects act, and objects are acted upon. If Othello is the protagonist of the play, then he's also the subject, and he's responsible for his own actions. He's a dignified character who has *agency*, the power to act. If *Iago* is the protagonist of the play, then Othello is just an *object*—a pawn, or maybe a *tool*—and he is *less* dignified and has *less* power. Do we understand what I'm talking about when I say dignity? I'm talking about his humanity. If Othello is responsible for his own decisions, he's more human, and if not, then he's been robbed of his humanity—he's been dehumanized. This is an important distinction to make, and an important question to ask about ourselves. Are we the subjects of our own lives, or are we objects? Are we protagonists of our own stories, or objects in other people's?"

The silence I was met with now was different from the one I'd faced at the beginning of the class. My students' brows were furrowed, their heads cocked sideways. They were thinking.

At last a hand came up—Adrienne's—but I waved it down. "We're not going to talk about it," I said. "We're going to write. Grab some paper and a pencil or pen. The question at hand is..." I uncapped my marker again and began to write on the board as I spoke.

If Othello is the protagonist of the play, he must be responsible for his own downfall. If so, what is his fault that we readers can learn from?

I turned back around. "If you guys want to argue someone or something *other* than Othello is responsible, go for it, but make sure you can explain yourselves and defend your answers. We'll write for—" I looked back up at the clock. "About twelve, maybe fifteen minutes. Then when we're finished, we'll have some time leftover for discussion."

ALLISON YOUNGER, at the coffee shop, gave me a funny look as she pushed my paper cup across the counter to me.

"Yes?"

"It's nothing. Stupid question."

I hit her with the teacher's standard response to such a statement.

After first appearing reticent, she looked up at me, full in the face. "Some of the kids are saying they saw you down at the river last weekend. You weren't walking down the middle of the river last Friday night, were you?"

I affected an expression of consideration. "What time on Friday night?"

"After midnight? Closer to one?"

"Were *you* down at the river last weekend, after midnight, closer to one?"

She blushed, looked away. "No, but..."

"Maybe it was just someone who looked like me," I suggested. "Or my ghost. I do haunt some of my former students sometimes."

pril became May. For a few afternoons, we had a taste of the ninety-degree weather that would scorch the plains over the summer, and then an overcast day and a night of rain washed the heat away. The spring sports teams moved from their regular seasons into their conference and regional schedules. The counselors sent their annual "I know it's late in the semester, but for the sake of numbers we need..." emails, which in some cases I answered positively, and in others I ignored completely. As if blown out by the Western Kansas wind, our pot smoking epidemic ended as abruptly and inexplicably as it had begun. Shakespeare's *Othello* behind us, I assigned my students research presentations instead of papers—an abbreviated assignment I had found in Gramley's book. The topic I assigned was broad: "Problems We Face in the World and People Who are Trying to Solve Them." Marcos presented on sustainable forms of protein for human consumption. Adrienne on agricultural water conservation. Javi talked to his peers about suitable compensation arrangements for collegiate athletes, with an emphasis on football players.

The semester raced to its conclusion. Twenty days became fifteen. Fifteen became ten. The seniors took their final exams and, to a chorus of cheers and airhorn blasts, walked across a stage set up on the football field's west end zone. With five days remaining for underclassmen, I delivered my last lectures and handed out study guides; then my juniors were taking their own finals. The semester ended.

I was grading the last of my exams on the last teacher workday before the summer break when my classroom phone rang. The readout said it was the front office. "They need you in the Principals' Conference Room, honey," said Nina, the office secretary.

I looked at the clock. It wasn't yet nine. "Do they need me now? Or is this something I can come in for later?"

"Now, honey."

"Do I need to bring anything?"

"Just yourself, unless you know somethin' I don't."

I stood up and took the long walk. The overhead lights off, the hallways were dim and my footfalls echoed. Unsure of what to expect, I was surprised to see not *principals,* plural, but only one, Mr. Russel, in the room. Beside him at the end of the conference table were Mrs. Hirsche and a man in a navy suit who it took me a moment to place: Steve Browning, the district HR director. As ever, the room seemed too small, and its windows looking out at the world too narrow, to be a place where decisions about children and their educations should take place. "Mr. Able," Mr. Russel said. "Good morning. Have a seat."

"Good morning," I returned. I pulled out the chair nearest the door. "Is there something I can help you with?"

Mrs. Hirsche snorted. "'Help' might be the operable word," she quipped. "We're here to talk about your continued employment."

I nodded. There was a list of teacher names—ten or eleven, at least, with Mrs. Rosenbaum, Mrs. Dennison, and Valerie Stephens among them—on the room's dull white marker board. Mine was at the top.

"I'd like my employment to be continued," I said as brightly as I could manage.

Mrs. Hirsche squinted. "Earlier this year you told me we'd be doing you a favor if we let you go."

I took a breath, exhaled. "You might. But I'm willing to do you guys a favor and stay." I smiled. Across from me, Mr. Russel also smiled. Mrs. Hirsche and Mr. Browning did not. "You earned five discipline citations this year," she said. "We're looking for someone who can be a team player."

"More than ninety percent of my students passed the state reading tests," I said. "I put up a lot of points for the team."

Mrs. Hirsche frowned; I sensed the sports metaphor she had introduced might be a difficult one for her to continue working with. Mr. Russel leaned in. "We're planning to further tighten the English department curriculum next year." His look was not unkind—might even have been encouraging. "We need team players who can put up points without earning penalties. Players who might be able to help lead."

I looked to Mrs. Hirsche. "You're thinking about rein-stating the department head position? And you want me to do it?"

Mrs. Hirsche shot a dirty look at Mr. Russel before glancing back to me. The creases on either side of her frown deepened. "We're not here to talk about scoring points or appointing department heads. We're here to talk about *trust*, and forming teams that *function*. We're here to talk about letting you *go*."

"Are you firing me?"

Mr. Browning cleared his throat and leaned in. "We're offering you the chance to resign."

I knew some things, from dinner table conversations with my father, about offered chances to resign.

"Or fall in line and teach the curriculum with greater fidelity," Mr. Russel hurried to add.

"And you'll hire someone new. Some first-year teacher who doesn't know the district and doesn't know the kids."

"Or someone with experience who can follow directions."

I looked to Mr. Russel and Mr. Browning to check for their responses to this, but neither of these men would meet my eye. "So a new curriculum," I said after a moment. "Something more in-line with the Gramley text."

The two men each looked up. They didn't seem to know what I was talking about.

"Stories Don't Matter in the Real World."

"It's our chief mentor-text for the curricular realignment." Mrs. Hirsche explained.

"And you need someone to be a team player who can fall in line and also lead." I knocked on the table. "That's me. I loved Gramley's book. I can be your point man. If you have some Continuing Ed funds and want to pick up copies for everyone in the department, I could lead a book study on it next fall."

I saw a grimace of uncertainty—or was it fear?—flicker across Mrs. Hirsche's face, but Mr. Russel was beaming. "We wouldn't need to go to District for Continuing Ed. I could use building funds to get copies. You'd be willing?"

"Absolutely."

He clapped his hands and looked back and forth to his neighbors. "Well then?"

Mr. Browning seemed to be relieved to have at least one meeting out of the way. Mrs. Hirsche looked as if a meal she'd been looking forward to had disappointed her, but grudgingly gave her assent. Mr. Russel stood to offer his hand across the table. "We'll see you in August," he said.

I told him I'd look forward to it.

WALKING BACK down the empty hallway to my classroom, I was visited by my perennial end-of-the-year memory: the Friday of Finals week, my senior year of college. I had already walked across the stage the previous weekend and was showing up now for an afternoon exam, the last time slot of the semester. The campus was all but deserted, and Davis and some of my other friends were waiting for me at a bar a few blocks away. The test would be a written one, in essay format, and the material was matter that I knew more or less cold. I had an 'A' in the class and was unlikely to lose it, but on the whole I hadn't performed as well in college or achieved as highly as I had expected. All of my rejection letters had come in, and there was nothing I could do to change the immediate trajectory of my life. I didn't seem to *have* a trajectory in my life. For the first time, something was ending, and I wouldn't be ascending to a new, higher plane when it was over. I had failed.

It was this same feeling of failure I had been visited with at the end of each school year since I had begun teaching. Because as each of my first three years had passed, I hadn't made it any closer to achieving my goal of returning to that higher plane of higher education—or advancing to any other plane. And because as each of those years had passed, I had failed to hit the reading and writing targets I and the district had set for my students. I had yet to even finish moving all the way through my curriculum. My students still read below level—several of them had made it through the year without doing much of the reading I had assigned —and many still wrote simple, unsophisticated sentences, omitting or misplacing commas and mixing up words like "saw" and "seen" and "imply" and "infer." They struggled to articulate formal arguments and left out apostrophes almost entirely.

I sat down at my desk and finished grading this latest group's exams, taking notes on the most common mistakes I encountered. A list that, though not dissimilar from that of the previous year, might have been a little shorter. Then I entered my exam scores, clipped the tests together, and dropped them into a drawer in case anyone came back with questions about theirs in the fall. I read over the list of final grades for my class one more time, and pushed the 'complete' button in my electronic grade book to send the scores to the registrar. And then I was finished.

I stood up, gave my room a last once-over, and picked up my bag. Outside, a district facilities crew was cutting the grass—clippings were scattered across the sidewalk—and this, too, was powerfully reminiscent of my last day of college: the long walk from the hall where I had taken my last final down to the student village where I would meet my friends. The heat and the smell of cut grass, the flowers blooming in the buildings' window boxes, the way I'd felt I had done a great deal of work but hadn't really accomplished—

But no matter. My list of student errors had been shorter

this year than last. And I had moved farther through the banned curriculum than I had ever moved through the curriculum when it was allowed. I would continue to work. We would continue to grow. I would meet my students— and the district's administration—head-on in the fall. Until then... Summer.

ACKNOWLEDGMENTS

I should first mention Michael Chabon and Richard Russo, whose campus novels *Wonder Boys* and *Straight Man* made me want to write my own 'campus' novel about a high school teacher in Western Kansas.

A number of books on writing helped me write this novel, chief among them *On Becoming a Novelist* by John Gardner, *Bird by Bird* by Anne Lamott, *The Modern Library Writer's Workshop* by Stephen Koch, *The Writer's Notebook Volumes I* and *II* from *Tin House Books*, *The Hidden Machinery* by Margot Livesey, *Wired for Story* by Lisa Cron, and *The Artful Edit* by Susan Bell.

At Kansas State University, Steve Heller and Susan Jackson Rodgers taught creative writing workshops that provided me a kind of creative and intellectual nourishment I desperately needed at the time.

I hope that I will not be confused with the protagonist of my book (and I certainly hope that my father, who is not a lawyer and does not live at a country club, will not be confused with William's father!), but I, too, have been a professional high school teacher who stumbled into the profession through a back door and learned lessons the hard way. A great deal of what I learned came from wonderful classroom teachers like Karan Long, Kay Daugaard, Wendi Terpstra, and Shelli Lalicker. New and would-be English teachers who are looking for helpful books on the craft of teaching would do well to start with works by practitioners like Kelly Gallagher, Nancy Atwell, and Jeffrey Wilhelm.

A number of friends have helped me by reading drafts of this book and allowing me to bounce ideas off of them. Chief among them are Anna Nelson and Kristin Huang, who read my first draft when it was almost twice as long as the book in your hands, and Sara Sedgwick, Ashley Agre, Madeline Byrd, and Nicole Porter. I particularly thank Sara Sedgwick, my classroom neighbor and friend, for her patience, knowledge, and good humor. My English department was kind enough to let me do my first-ever 'reading' and Q&A at an inservice meeting—I thank them!

The poet Taylor Mali responded with open-handed generosity when I wrote him a letter requesting the use of a few of his words in my epigraph; his poem "What Teachers Make" was a partial germ for this book, and his poetry helped me sprout a pretty successful classroom career, to boot. I think everyone should read his work.

Meg Storey helped me developmentally edit this novel. Without the many pages of notes she gave me when the book was in the 3rd-person, I wouldn't have had the courage to tear it down, reimagine it, and spend fourteen months writing this much tighter, more narratively-cohesive and successful version.

(I hired neither a copywriter nor proofreader for this book; any typos, clunky word choices, or infelicities of style are mine entirely.)

Maurice Olin walked up to me at the end of class one day and handed me a pencil sketch: teacher treasure; manna from the heavens. Nathaniel Roy used that sketch and made a cover that I am absolutely in love with. I am tremendously grateful to them both.

I'm lucky to have grown up in a house of books, magazines, newspapers, and music. Great thanks to my mother for raising me to love art, literature, and culture, and my father for raising me to love physical puzzles, word puzzles, and wit. (What else is a novel but a giant puzzle and word puzzle that hopefully contains some wit?)

Finally, my wife, Esther has also read several versions of this book, but more importantly has been my loving and supportive partner in this life. Along with our two sons, Jonathan and William, she has enriched my experience of this world and thereby enriched my fiction. Esther, Jonathan, and William, I love and thank you!

Acknowledgments, continued:

You're still here?

You're right: I did forget someone. I want to thank *you*, dear reader. Writers like me *need* readers like you. I aspire to write a slower, more 'literary' brand of fiction than much of what I see as popular today. My writing isn't for everyone—I'm glad you enjoyed it. This book is self-published. I wrote it, rewrote it, and rewrote it again. I hired a real human editor, paid a real human artist for the cover art and the sketches embedded in the online serial version, and I hired a real human cover designer. I created an 'llc' and started my own publishing house: lower midlist publishing. My book has not been anointed by the literary agents in New York, the big traditional publishing houses, or even one of the nimble little houses. It has not enjoyed the benefits of those entities' marketing budgets or connections. The fact that so many people like you have taken to reading it heartens me and gratifies me immensely. If you'd like to read more of my work, you can subscribe to my newsletter at https://substack.com/@pshull. If you enjoyed my book and would like to do me the favor of supporting me, it's as easy as leaving a positive written review online or making use of your own personal social network to connect my book with more wise, attractive, searching, and generous readers like yourself.

Stay tuned: I have a couple more books coming in the next few years—a whole "Kansas" trilogy, in fact! We won't be talking about teachers and students anymore...

～

Forthcoming: *Komojo!: a Tale of Online Adventure and Real-World Mistakes.*